Demon Hunters 6: Feud

Demon Hunters 6
Feud

Avril Sabine

Cracked Acorn Productions
Australia

Demon Hunters 6: Feud

Published by

Cracked Acorn Productions

PO Box 1365

Gympie, Queensland 4570

Australia

978-1-925617-54-2 (Kindle)

978-1-925617-55-9 (EPUB)

978-1-925617-56-6 (Print)

Genre: Young Adult Urban/Fantasy/Horror

Cover design by Caitlyn Petersen

*For my youngest, who tells me he's my
number one fan. But not to be worried about
that.*

Aura spends a ridiculous amount of time rescuing her mum from dangerous situations. This one would have to be the worst. More dangerous than the serial killer episode. And for once, it isn't her mum's fault. Not that it makes the situation any less dangerous or the chance of her survival any greater. Demons are real and they want her family dead. She's determined not to let that happen. Now if only she can come up with a sensible plan. One that will allow her and her family to live.

*

This story was written by an Australian author using Australian spelling.

Chapter One

Aura tried the air-conditioner again. Only hot air poured from the vents, competing with the warm air already flowing into the car from the open windows. She glared at her mum. "If you had pulled into the mechanics at the last town instead of telling me 'bubble it' we might not be melting right now."

Hazel smiled serenely. "It was trying to rain. We didn't need the air-con." She glanced at Aura. "I keep telling you if you'd join me in putting our problems in a bubble and releasing them into the universe, they'd solve themselves."

Aura sighed heavily. She should know by now that nothing would convince her mum that whatever current strange fad she was following wouldn't work. As always, it'd be left to her to deal with the practicalities. "We could have at least stopped and asked for directions." Giving up on the air-conditioner, she stared at the windy road and rolling hills ahead of them. The narrow road, barely wide enough for two vehicles to pass, was deserted and it had been kilometres since they'd passed a house. Not that she was certain anyone had lived in the dilapidated dwelling.

"Zinnia said we wouldn't be able to miss Blue Sky Community," Hazel said.

Aura opened her mouth to once more comment on the name of the place. It sounded like a commune to her. Shaking her head, she closed her mouth. Her mum would probably give her another one of her serene smiles and tell her to 'bubble it' and change the subject. Her gaze remained on her mum, trying to figure out how they could be so unalike when they looked so similar. She had her mum's dark brown eyes and similar facial features with a small nose and oval face. The only difference was her mum had light brown hair while hers was honey gold, a legacy from her father, a surfer her mum had met one summer. As always, she came to no conclusion. At least no logical one. She certainly wasn't going to start coming up with illogical ones like her mum did.

Hazel glanced at Aura. "I'm sure we're nearly there. Zinnia said it was only an hour from that last town."

"We've driven for more than an hour," Aura pointed out.

"Of course we have. It takes longer to arrive somewhere the first time."

Aura opened her mouth only to close it again, looking out the window. They came around a corner to see a young man pushing a motorbike along the side of the road, a helmet hanging from the handlebar and his shirt off. It was wrapped around his head against the afternoon sun that hadn't cooled any even though night was less than a couple of hours away.

Hazel slowed the car, pulling over to the side of the road in front of him. "See if he needs a lift somewhere."

"Mum." She kept her voice low, worried her words would carry to the young man who'd leaned his motorbike against a tree and was walking towards her window, visible in the side mirror of her door. "Keep driving. Are you insane?"

"What do you mean?"

It was too late. The young man leaned forward to peer in the car, grinning as he removed the shirt from his head to reveal sandy blond hair, short at the back and sides with a little more length at the front.

"I didn't think I'd be lucky enough to have

someone come along this road. Not much out this way." He held his hand out. "I'm Riley Hunter."

Aura eyed his hand, wanting to move away. Which was impossible since she was as far back in her seat as she could get. Sunlight caught on the cross at his neck, but she wasn't reassured by the sight of it. He was too tall, around six foot, and his wiry muscles let her know he'd be a lot stronger than her. She noticed he had a silver stud, in the shape of a cross, in one ear before her gaze was caught by warm brown eyes.

Hazel leaned forward to take his hand. "I'm Hazel and this is my daughter Aura. Are you from Blue Sky Community?"

Aura was watching him carefully enough she noticed the momentary wariness that entered his eyes.

"I'm staying with Colin and Judy who live up the road from them. If you can give me a lift as far as Blue Sky I'd appreciate it."

"We don't have room for your bike," Aura said.

Riley's smile didn't falter. "That's okay. I'll hide it and the helmet behind some of the bushes along the side of the road and borrow Colin's ute to pick it up later. Not many people come along this road so it would probably be okay if I didn't hide it."

"Don't be silly," Hazel said. "As if we'd make you walk in this heat. We'll drop you where you're staying. Hop in the back."

Aura reached for the door handle, speaking quickly. "I'll get in the back. You can show my mum where you live."

Riley chuckled as he stepped back from the door she was opening. "Want to check me over for weapons?"

She looked him up and down as she got out of the car. He seemed even taller standing beside her. "Do I need to?"

His smile faded. "It isn't me you should be wary of." His voice was soft enough it wouldn't have carried to Hazel.

She kept her voice equally low. "You say that like you know who I should be wary of."

"Why are you going to Blue Sky?"

"Mum's sister moved there a few months back. She's been asking us to join them ever since." There was no way she was about to let her mum visit some dodgy sounding commune on her own. Who knew what trouble she'd get into.

Riley continued to meet her gaze, eventually taking a step back and gesturing towards his motorbike. "Give me a minute."

She watched him stride away, frowning as she tried to figure out what had happened. Did he know something about Blue Sky? She remained by the back door, watching as he slung his shirt over a shoulder and wheeled the motorbike further away from the edge of the road, hiding it behind some of the bushes.

Riley started back towards the car, grinning as he slipped his arms into his button up shirt, the long sleeves remaining rolled up. He nodded towards the front seat. "Still want me to sit in the front?" He buttoned the shirt as he waited for her answer.

Her attention was caught by a tattoo that wrapped around his left wrist more than twice, a narrow black line with a hint of red in it that started at his pulse point. "What does that mean?" She gestured to it.

Riley rolled down his sleeves. "Depends on who you ask."

"I thought I asked you."

Riley glanced skywards. "Should make a move before night comes."

She opened her mouth to ask him another question, closing it, question unasked. She might as well have been trying to get her mum to focus on a topic with how much luck she was having getting information out of him. "You can sit in the front."

She waited until he was in the car before she got in the back, keeping an eye on him.

Hazel checked over her shoulder before pulling onto the narrow road. "How far are you past Blue Sky?"

"A few kilometres," Riley said.

"I thought you said just up the road."

Riley turned in his seat to meet Aura's gaze. "It is. By rural standards." He grinned. "Colin and Judy are neighbours. Their property adjoins Blue Sky along one side."

"Are they family?" Hazel asked. "Colin and Judy."

"No."

"Friends?" Hazel glanced at Riley.

He shook his head. "I've been helping them."

"Oh, you work for them," Hazel said.

Riley shrugged. "That's one way of putting it."

Aura wanted to demand how he'd put it, but her mum was asking him about the area and how long he was staying with Colin and Judy. She was tempted to point out to her mum that he tended to avoid actually answering the questions and that they'd learned pretty much nothing about him. His words came back to her. If he wasn't the one she should be worried about, then why was he being so secretive while seemingly being open with his casual comments and ready smiles?

Riley pointed to a large sign coming up on the right. "That's Blue Sky."

It was a hand painted sign with uneven lettering on a blue background. Aura turned in her seat to watch it as they drove past. Her expectations for the place plummeted further. Was it too late to convince her aunt to leave immediately? Zinnia was supposedly the sensible one of the two sisters. How had she been conned into moving here?

The car jerked to one side and Hazel gasped.

Aura grabbed hold of the handle above the door. "What happened?"

"Flat tyre." Hazel slowed the car and pulled over onto the side of the road.

Aura sighed heavily. She should have known. Everything else that could possibly go wrong had. Unbuckling her seat belt, she opened the door, eyeing the angled area they were parked on. "It keeps getting better," she muttered.

Riley got out of the car and walked around to the driver's side. "Do you have a spare?"

Hazel joined him. "It's in the boot. Under all our things."

Aura leaned back in the seat, closing her eyes. All

the things her mum had said didn't need packing in bags. Hers were packed into two bags, a small one and a mid sized one. The rest of the gear was scattered throughout the boot in her mum's usual haphazard fashion. After another sigh she opened her eyes before clambering out of the car to join Riley where he stood staring at the contents in the boot. His expression had her tempted to laugh, but there was nothing at all amusing about the situation. Movement caught her attention and she turned to watch her mum.

Hazel made a circling motion with her hands. "Bubble it." She then pushed something away from her. Something no one could see.

Aura clamped her teeth together, desperately trying not to comment.

"What does that mean?" Riley nodded towards Hazel, keeping his voice low so only Aura heard him.

"You really don't want to know."

Riley grinned. "I don't tend to ask questions unless I want to know the answer to them, sweetheart."

"I'm not your sweetheart." Her gaze narrowed.

"Aura."

Not that she liked her name any better than being called sweetheart.

"Interesting name."

"Yeah well, Mum was going through an aura reading stage when I was born. At least she'd moved past the palm reading stage by then. Who knows what I might have been called otherwise."

"Heart line?"

She liked that as little as her current name. Then she would have been called sweetheart. "Fate?" She glanced at him when he chuckled.

"That seems a likely choice." He nodded towards the contents of the boot. "Have you got anything to put some of this gear in?"

Chapter Two

Aura searched through the boot until she found a towel. "We could bundle some of the stuff in this."

Hazel joined them at the boot. "I'll walk to the corner so I can warn any oncoming traffic that we're here."

Aura opened her mouth to argue, or ask why she didn't let the universe take care of it. She closed her mouth instead. It'd probably be easier without her mum's help.

"We've got it," Riley said.

Hazel smiled serenely, took a straw hat from the boot and wandered down the road.

Aura watched her leave for a moment before turning back to the boot, gesturing towards the mess. "Sorry about all this."

"Ah well, a challenge is always good for one's

character." Riley chuckled. " Or so my gran keeps telling me."

Her gaze was drawn to him, surprised by his comment. "You visit your gran?" That didn't seem like the kind of thing a serial killer would do. Although what would she know about normal? She did know a little bit about serial killers though.

"My cousins and I lived with her until recently." Riley gathered some of the clothes scattered throughout the boot and dumped them in the middle of the towel.

"You and your cousins? Where are your parents?" She added more to the pile on the towel before bundling it up.

"Europe."

She'd taken half a step away from the boot before he'd spoken, stopping to face him. "Europe? Why are they in Europe?"

"Work." He nodded towards the towel. "Do you have another one? Or something else we can use?"

She dumped the bundle on the back seat, gathering her bags next and putting them on the floor in the back, having no idea what to use for the rest of her mum's things. She stared at the mess in the boot. "I'm not sure what to use. Maybe we'll have to keep using the towel and tip everything onto the back seat."

It didn't take long to ditch all the gear on the back seat, once they'd settled on a plan, and Riley took the tyre out setting it beside the back driver's side before looking for the jack. "You're not much alike, you and your mum." He knelt beside the flat tyre and loosened the wheel nuts before jacking the car up.

"That's an understatement." She took the flat tyre he removed and put it in the boot before beginning to gather all the gear off the back seat. Once they were done, she closed the boot and leaned against the car to look at Riley. "Are you collecting your bike this arve?"

"As long as it's before dark." He glanced skywards.

She was tempted to ask him what happened after dark, but it probably wasn't important. Not that he was likely to answer given his previous avoidance of most of their questions. "I can give you a hand." She gestured towards the tyre he'd replaced. "I bet you didn't think you'd be stuck changing a tyre on a hot day like this." She'd still have been changing it if she'd had her mum's help.

Riley wiped his hands on his jeans. "It's okay. I was happy to help, sweetheart."

She gave him a look to let him know she wasn't happy with being called sweetheart.

He grinned. "Aura."

"Do you call everyone that?"

"Pretty much." He glanced in the direction Hazel had taken. "Want to call your mum so we can get out of this heat? I doubt the day is going to cool off any time soon."

She walked around to the driver's door and put her hand in the open window to sound the horn. Facing him, she met his gaze. "I will help you." While she watched him, he once more glanced skywards and she couldn't resist asking the question she'd avoided earlier. "What's your problem with the sun setting?"

Riley smiled. "I never said I had a problem with it."

"No, but you seem pretty focused on when the day will end."

He glanced along the road. "Your mum is on the way back." He walked around the car to the passenger door.

She glared at his retreating figure. According to him he might not have a problem with the day ending, but he certainly did have one with answering questions.

Hazel reached the car, smiling. "That didn't take long and nothing came along. The universe took care of everything."

Her jaw tightened as she clamped down on the argumentative words she wanted to speak. They wouldn't make a difference. Getting in the car, she glanced skywards when she noticed Riley did so. There was probably less than an hour left in the day.

Hazel started the car, pulling back onto the road. "How much further is it to the place you're staying at?" She glanced at Riley.

"Only a couple of corners away," Riley said.

"I'm going to help Riley get his bike. I'll meet you at Blue Sky after we finish collecting it."

Hazel momentarily met her gaze in the rear view mirror. "That's lovely. It'll give me time to catch up with Zinnia. It has to have been a month since I last saw her."

"More like three months," Aura said.

"Are you sure?" Hazel once more briefly met her gaze in the rear view mirror.

"Yes, Mum. I'm sure."

"The driveway is just up there." Riley pointed to a gravel drive, large ruts at the start of it, equally deep ones scattered along it. "You might want to drop me here rather than attempt the driveway in your car."

"I'm sure I can manage to get you to the house," Hazel said.

Aura eyed the driveway. It had to be a hundred metres long, a dilapidated Queenslander at the end of it. From what she could see, the driveway didn't improve as it neared the house. If anything, there were larger ruts. "I could do with a walk after being in the car for so long." She could also do without something under the car breaking.

Hazel pulled up, looking over her shoulder. "Are you sure?"

Aura opened the car door. "Yeah." She half stepped out. "I'll see you once we get the bike back here."

Hazel smiled serenely. "It'll be nice to catch up with Zinnia."

She started to comment on Blue Sky, but at the last second changed her mind. The words wouldn't make a difference. She'd only be wasting her breath. "Yeah." Once she was out of the car, she closed the door and stood beside Riley, waving to her mum as she drove back the way they'd come.

Riley met her gaze. "I'm surprised you offered to help."

She was too, but she didn't tell him that. She didn't usually trust people easily. Especially not good looking guys with ready smiles. But she owed him for his help. Shrugging, she nodded towards the house where a ute was parked close to the sagging verandah. The ute looked to be in as good a condition as the house and driveway. "You sure the ute will hold together long enough to pick up the bike?"

Riley chuckled, starting along the driveway. "Guess we'll find out soon enough."

His words weren't reassuring, but she walked at his side, stepping around the larger ruts, her gaze drawn to a few she was certain would have caused damage to the car. "How long are you staying with Colin and Judy?" Even though her mum had asked, he hadn't really given a clear answer. She was determined to get him to answer at least one question about himself. Properly answer it and not give some vague or unrevealing comment.

"Hopefully I'll be back in Brisbane before uni starts back at the beginning of next month."

She stumbled on one of the ridges leading into a rut. "You're at uni?"

Riley glanced at her with a grin. "Not what you expected of a serial killer?"

"I never said you were a serial killer."

"Actions speak louder than words."

A wry smile formed. "Can you blame me?"

"Not at all, sweetheart."

"How would you like it if I started calling you sweetheart?"

"Go ahead. It's only fair after all."

She glanced at him several times, not sure if he was serious. "You won't mind if I call you sweetheart."

She glanced at him when he didn't speak, her only answer a grin. "Fine. Sweetheart."

Riley laughed.

Aura stumbled on the edge of a rut, distracted by the sound, trying to figure out how the conversation had wandered away from the original topic. "How did you end up here?"

"One of my cousins dropped me off."

"Why?"

"Because Colin and Judy needed a hand."

She frowned. Nothing made sense. "What about your motorbike?"

"It's Colin's. Or at least it belongs to one of his sons who now lives in Brisbane."

"You don't have a vehicle here?"

Riley shrugged. "I didn't expect to stay so long and Emily and Dan had to go back to Brisbane yesterday. They had other things to deal with."

"Your cousins?"

"Emily is my cousin." He flashed her another grin. "What's with the interrogation?"

"What was with avoiding the questions my mum asked?"

They reached the ute as the front screen door opened, an old man remaining in the doorway. His skin was leathery and wrinkled, only wisps of hair remaining on his head. He wore a faded checked shirt, his trousers equally faded and held up on his narrow frame with a worn leather belt.

"You didn't put the bike in a ditch, did you?"

Riley grinned. "Didn't you believe me when I told you I could ride?"

"Not with the way you tore out of here."

Riley chuckled, turning to Aura. "This is Colin." He looked towards the old man. "Colin, this is Aura. She's visiting next door, along with her mother."

Colin's expression changed. "What are you doing bringing her here?"

Aura nearly took a step back at the venom she heard in his voice. "Riley helped change a flat tyre for us. I'm returning the favour by helping him collect the bike."

"Don't need help from any of you hippies." Colin came to the edge of the verandah, letting the screen door slam shut behind him. "I'll give you a hand to get the bike."

"It's okay, Colin. They're not moving in. Aura has an aunt there."

Colin leaned against the verandah railing. "They should all go back to where they came from. Never trusted that Curtis. Always believed there was something not right about him."

"You've got good instincts, Colin. Don't let prejudices get in the way of them," Riley said.

"The lot of them are as bad as that Curtis."

"There might be more than one wolf living next door, but the majority of them are lambs." Riley gestured towards the ute. "I better get going before it's dark."

"Don't matter how many of them are lambs. They mess with wolves they deserve what's coming to them." Colin returned inside, the screen door slamming shut behind him.

Aura stared into the shadowy interior of the house. "What was that all about?"

Riley strode to the ute, glancing over his shoulder. "You coming?"

She went around to the passenger side of the ute, the door creaking loudly. "You don't much like answering questions." She sat on the cracked vinyl of the bench seat, glad she was wearing jeans. Earlier, when the air conditioner had failed, she'd regretted putting them on.

Riley started the engine and the vehicle struggled to life with a shudder. "People don't always want an answer when they ask a question. Or at least they don't want to hear the answer."

She grabbed hold of the armrest on the door as the

ute shuddered and rattled down the driveway. "Are you sure this thing won't fall apart before we get to the road?"

Riley laughed. "I'll say a few prayers that it gets us back in one piece."

She stared at him. "You pray?"

"I don't wear a cross for decoration."

"I didn't think normal people believed in religion anymore." She let go of the handle when they reached the road and it stopped feeling like she was being shaken apart.

Riley glanced at her, grinning. "Are you sure I'm normal?"

"Not at all." She couldn't help glancing at the sign for Blue Sky Community as they drove past. "What is Colin's problem with them?"

"Things haven't been right in the area since Curtis arrived. The place was up for sale, but it was taken off the market and Curtis moved in."

"What's wrong with that? Maybe they decided to rent it out because it wasn't selling."

Riley glanced at her, not saying a word.

"What?"

"I didn't say anything."

"But you wanted to."

"People don't always say everything they think."

She couldn't exactly argue that. Not when she had a tendency to keep most of her thoughts to herself. The silence stretched out awkwardly, broken only by the sounds of the ute. "What are you studying at uni?"

"Psychology. How about you? Have you finished school? Going on to uni? Have other plans?"

Chapter Three

Aura studied him. Psychology? He didn't seem the type. But then she didn't really know him. Who knew what his ready smiles hid. For a few seconds she began to wonder at her sanity for having decided to help him. She pushed those worries aside. It was too late to be concerned about it now. "I finished year twelve last year. I'm doing veterinary science. There are always more positions available for vets than there are applicants to fill them."

"You're going to base the direction of your life on job availability."

"At least I'll be able to afford to live." And not have to worry about numerous sudden moves due to rent not being paid on time. Or empty cupboards because no groceries had been bought because there was no money for them.

Riley slowed, doing a three-point turn in a spot

halfway between two corners. "Maybe I should give you my number for when job dissatisfaction gets to you later in life and you find yourself needing help to figure out where you went wrong."

"Doing things because they sound fun and interesting doesn't work." Life had taught her that repeatedly. A pity her mum hadn't learned the lesson.

He drove back towards Colin's place for a few metres. "The key to life is balance." He pulled up, parking on the side of the road, the ground angling away from the bitumen. "It doesn't have to be one or the other."

Her jaw tightened. He didn't know what he was talking about. Opening the door, she got out instead of bothering to reply. Once the motorbike was back at Colin's place she'd probably never see him again. Scanning the bushes along the side of the road, she tried to spot the motorbike. It was too well hidden.

Riley strode around to the back of the ute, unstrapping the planks on the tray. He slid them into place before heading for a clump of bushes and bringing the motorbike out, the helmet hanging from the handlebar.

When he started up the ramps, the motorbike on one plank, Riley on the other, she moved behind the motorbike and pushed against the seat. The ramps were on a sharp angle, the motorbike an effort to push up them. "Lucky the planks were on the ute."

Riley finished pushing the motorbike up onto the tray. "Not the first time the bike has returned home on the ute."

She held the motorbike while Riley strapped it into place and put the planks back, strapping them on too.

He glanced skywards.

She did the same. The sun was low on the horizon, the sky filled with colour. "That's one thing you rarely see in the city." The vibrant colours reminded her of the year her mum had taken up painting, spending far too much money to learn that all she was capable of doing was splashing colours across the canvas. When her mum quit the instructor had claimed, that unlike her mum, she had a natural talent and had tried to convince her to continue attending lessons. But someone had to be practical. The money her mum had made as a waitress hadn't been enough to cover unnecessary things.

"We better get going before it's dark." Riley jumped off the tray of the ute, landing on the driver's side, taking the helmet with him.

Aura remained on the tray. "What is your problem with the night?"

Riley gestured along the road. "I don't know if

you've noticed, but we're not exactly in the city out here. No streetlights and kilometres between houses."

Once again he'd avoided the question. Not exactly saying that was his problem, only insinuating. She remained on the back of the ute, watching him before clambering off. He was already in the ute, starting the engine as soon as she closed the door, the helmet between them on the seat. The vinyl creaked as she tried to get comfortable on the aged seat, the noise competing with all the other ones.

"I'll drive up to the next clear stretch before I turn around and then drop you at Blue Sky before I return to Colin and Judy's place," Riley said.

"Who will help you get the bike off the tray?"

"There's enough flat ground around the house it won't be a problem." Riley slowed for several kangaroos that jumped out onto the road ahead of them, hitting the horn and coming to a stop when they froze, staring at the ute.

One of the kangaroos rose to his full height and Aura stared at him, glad she was in the ute and not standing in front of him. He towered over them, the other kangaroos gathered around him. "Why aren't they moving?"

Riley rubbed at his wrist with the tattoo. "Guess they weren't expecting to find something on the road." He drove forward slowly, the animals remaining in place.

She leaned forward. "Shouldn't they move? We're just about on top of them."

Riley rubbed his wrist again. "You'd think." He grinned. "Maybe they're curious."

Drawing her gaze from the animals, she stared at Riley. He didn't appear as relaxed as he'd been earlier. "What's wrong?" Her gaze went from his face to his wrist and then back again. "Why do you keep rubbing your tattoo?"

Riley glanced over his shoulder. "I'll back up and try to go round them."

"There isn't enough room." She looked from one side of the narrow road to the other. "We'll end up in a gully."

"We can't sit here the rest of the day waiting for them to move." Riley backed up before heading forward again, glancing at the sky.

She glanced skywards too. The vibrant colours were fading, darkening. It was nearly night. Uneasiness settled deep within her. "They should be moving." Her words were quiet as she watched the kangaroos. When Riley started to go around them, the ute on an angle, she clutched the armrest, her grip tightening when the largest kangaroo moved towards them.

"Want to join me for dinner?" Riley continued past the animals and came back up on the road.

She stared out the back window, his words not sinking in immediately. Facing him, she frowned. "Dinner? At Colin and Judy's place."

Riley grinned. "I promise you're not on the menu."

"Can you promise no harm will come to me?"

"That depends. Are you a clumsy type of person?" He turned on the headlights.

"No."

"So what do you say? Dinner?"

"I don't know." She glanced over her shoulder, able to see very little in the last light of the day. What sort of trouble was her mum likely to end up in if she wasn't there to keep an eye on her?

"Judy is a good cook. She won't mind an extra."

"What about Colin? Won't he mind?"

Riley chuckled. "He'll tolerate you if he has no choice."

She stared at his profile, trying to figure out why he was inviting her. There was very little light by which to read his expression. The dash lights were dim. "Why are you inviting me?"

Riley glanced at her. "Wouldn't you like the chance to continue your interrogation?"

She couldn't shake the uneasiness from when the kangaroos had stopped in front of them. "Maybe you should take me back to Blue Sky."

He turned off the road and onto the rutted driveway. "Maybe isn't exactly no."

It wasn't until she clambered out of the ute, Riley parking it to face the driveway they'd come down, that she realised he hadn't answered her earlier question. Hadn't promised she wouldn't come to harm. He was out of the vehicle before she could lean back in to point it out. She hurried after him. The headlights that had been left on highlighted a figure walking towards them, seeming to have come out of nowhere. Her mouth gaped as the man came closer and she realised he must be close to seven foot tall. His shoulders were broad and he wore no shirt, enough muscles on display that he might have been a body builder.

"Go tell Judy we're back." Riley stepped in front of her.

"Who–"

"Hurry. She'll be worried since we're back so late."

Aura looked from the body builder to Riley, stepping to the side of Riley before she spoke. "Who is that?" She wasn't about to let him send her inside. She wanted to know what was going on.

Riley kept his voice low. "Someone you don't want to meet."

She noticed he again rubbed at his tattoo. "Should you call the police?" The screen door slammed behind her and she jumped, turning to see Colin on the verandah, carrying a rifle, the dim overhead light doing little to dispel the darkness in the yard. "Riley." She grabbed his arm, tugging in the hope he'd turn and see the weapon.

"It's okay. Go inside, sweetheart."

The endearment made her jaw tighten. "I am not your sweetheart."

"Aura." He glanced at her. "Go inside."

The sharp tone had her gaping again, closing her mouth with an audible sound. A glance over her shoulder showed Colin remained on the verandah. There was also a narrow figure at the screen door, highlighted by the light behind.

The man stopped in front of Riley, who once again had stepped in front of Aura. "I warned you."

Aura frowned at the smell of smouldering wood fire that seemed to come from the man.

"You are as welcome as you were last time and I can make your stay as short," Riley warned.

The man laughed. "You think I haven't planned for that? It was considerate of you to be in an area with those willing to make deals with my kind."

"It doesn't matter how many times you return I will continue to send you home," Riley said.

The man pointed directly at Riley. "I plan to live up to the name I was previously summoned by. Do you remember as clearly as I do?"

"Our encounter barely made an impression on me, Feud." Riley shrugged. "I guess it was more memorable for you than it was for me."

Aura wanted to demand if Riley was crazy. Goading someone who was nearly a foot taller than him and far broader was complete insanity.

"I see you at least remember my name. For all your insinuations I wasn't as forgettable as you'd have me believe. I'm sure you remember our encounter in the hospital car park as clearly as I do."

"Get off my property and back to where you belong," Colin shouted.

Aura looked over her shoulder to see the old man had his rifle pointed at Feud. She opened her mouth to demand what was going on. Feud spoke before she could.

"You think your puny weapon will bother me?"

"It'll do more than bother," Riley said. "Those

bullets will burn. Blessed and dipped. I can add my prayers to them as well."

"Are you crazy?" Aura demanded. "You think praying is going to help at a time like this?" He was obviously as impractical as her mum with the way she thought the universe would take care of her if she gave it her problems.

Feud looked past Riley. "A non believer. Why aren't you next door with the rest of them?"

Aura struggled not to step back, her attention caught by the flicker of light in his dark eyes. For a second she thought it was flames. Pushing aside the fanciful notion, she told herself it was the reflection of the headlights. "What have you got to do with Blue Sky?"

Feud grinned, the smell of smouldering fires increasing. "I'm very close friends with those at Blue Sky Community. Every single one of them would do anything for me." His gaze returned to Riley. "Absolutely anything I asked of them. Summoning, blood, anything."

The mild tone of his voice contradicted the intense look in his eyes and had Aura wanting to jump in the ute and race next door, grab her mum and aunt and head back to Brisbane. A gunshot had her jumping and she stared at the wound on Feud's torso, blood trickling down his body, appearing black in the headlights. Her mouth opened, but no words formed.

Feud remained standing, only a hiss indicating he'd felt the bullet.

"Get out of here," Colin called out. "Or I'll shoot you again."

Feud pointed at Colin. "They already want you gone. It'll be my pleasure to oblige them." He grinned, bringing his hands together in a loud clap. The headlights shattered, the area darkening.

Riley moved away, tossing a liquid at Feud who roared, grabbing hold of Aura's arm and dragging her towards the house with him.

She stumbled at his side, the uneven ground mostly shadows, the light on the verandah doing little to help. "What's-"

"Move it, sweetheart."

She stumbled up the four steps and onto the verandah. "What is-"

Riley pushed her towards the door where an elderly woman continued to stand. "Inside." He took a sword from the woman, spinning to face the yard.

"Better come inside, love." The woman stepped out of the doorway. "I'm Judy. I take it you're the young lady who was here earlier."

"What is going on?" She finally managed to get all the words out.

"Come inside." Judy's gnarled fingers wrapped around her wrist and drew her into the hallway. "You don't want to be out there." There was worry in her faded blue eyes, her silver hair drawn back from her face in a thin plait.

Chapter Four

Aura pulled out of Judy's grip. "I want to know what is going on." Turning, she looked outside, seeing Colin and Riley standing together on the verandah, Feud no longer in sight. "Where did he go?" Then it struck her. "I have to go. My mum is next door. And my aunt." The screen door banged shut behind her as she headed for the stairs.

Riley stepped in front of her, preventing her from leaving. "It isn't safe out there. Not yet."

She couldn't draw her gaze from the sword he held. "What is going on? And who are you?"

"I've already told you. Riley Hunter."

"That tells me nothing." She glared at him.

Riley grinned. "It actually tells you more than you realise."

Her hands curled into fists and she had the urge to hit him.

Riley's grin faded. "Stay the night."

"What? How did you make the leap from a dinner invitation to sleep over?"

"Simple. You really don't want to go out there, sweetheart."

"I'll finish making dinner," Judy said.

"Who is Feud?" Aura gestured to the area where the man had been standing. "And what does he want with you?"

"A better question would be what is Feud." Riley took a step around her. "Come inside."

She remained where she was, turning to face him, glancing at the screen door when it slammed shut. Colin had gone inside. She was alone on the verandah with Riley. "I'm not going anywhere until you tell me what is going on."

Riley took another step towards the screen door. "I doubt you'd believe me anyway."

"Try me." She crossed her arms over her chest, remaining where she was.

"Can we at least have this conversation inside?" Riley held the screen door open, propping his sword against the wall inside close by the door.

She remained on the verandah a few more seconds before she uncrossed her arms and strode inside, remaining by the door. "What is going on?"

"You're persistent."

"That doesn't tell me anything I don't already know."

"Come into the lounge room and I'll show you some photos."

"What sort of photos?" She took half a step towards him.

"They're in here." He moved back towards the first doorway off the hallway, a fancy timber panel above that had a flower shape cut into it. A glance along the hallway showed the other three doors had the same decorative panel above them.

She took a hesitant step forward, glancing towards the screen door and the exit. Not that it was safe outside. Feud could be anywhere. "What about my mum? I need to let her know I'm okay." She also needed to find out if her mum and aunt were safe. It wasn't like she could use her mobile phone in this area. She'd learned earlier, when the air-conditioner had failed to work, that there was no coverage.

"There's a phone in the lounge room." He entered the room, remaining near the doorway.

She stepped closer, her gaze scanning the room. A faded floral curtain hung at the window that overlooked the verandah, pulled shut against the night. Along that wall was a crowded bookcase, mostly filled with magazines and old framed photographs, an equally cluttered desk under the window, an old style phone sitting on the corner. She wasn't even certain if the bulky phone, with its rotary dial in the centre, would work.

Riley chuckled, his gaze also drawn to the phone. "The place probably hasn't been updated since the sixties when they moved in here as newlyweds."

Her gaze was drawn to the other end of the room where a lounge suite took up most of the space, the green of the cushions faded, the vinyl of the arms cracked and stained from years of use. They were clustered around a coffee table, the corners chipped and the laminate peeled away at the edges, the angled legs scuffed. Spread out on the table were numerous photos, the modernness of them seeming out of place in this room that appeared to have been caught in a time warp.

She crossed the space between her and the photos, sitting heavily on the nearest armchair when she saw the one on top. Her hand pressed against her mouth in an effort not to lose the contents of her stomach.

Riley crouched beside her, looking up with concern in his warm, brown eyes. "Are you okay?"

She gestured towards the image, keeping her other hand pressed against her mouth.

Riley flipped the image over, along with three others. "I thought you planned to be a vet."

She lowered her hand, her stomach still rebelling against what she'd seen. "Vets don't carve animals up like that." She tried to push the image from her mind. It was impossible. Blood, gore and what had once been a cow, recognisable only from the head, kept returning. "That's… that's…" Words failed her and she shook her head, gesturing towards the coffee table.

Riley captured her hand. "You should go home. Take your mum and aunt with you and return to Brisbane."

"What is going on here?" She had a good idea from some of the other ritualistic looking images on the coffee table, but she wanted him to tell her. Wanted to hear the words.

"Go home, Aura. There's nothing here for you."

"You're the one who wants me to stay the night."

Riley smiled fleetingly. "In the morning. Go and convince your family to leave with you."

Aura sighed heavily. "That might be a little more difficult than you think." Her mum would likely say 'bubble it', smile serenely and put it in the hands of the universe. She couldn't wait until her mum grew bored with her current fad. Not that there was any guarantee the next fad would be any better.

"Surely you can convince them it's not safe in this area."

She drew her hand from his, anger rising. "Why don't you try and convince them? And what about the rest of the people at Blue Sky? What about Colin and Judy? Shouldn't you be telling them to leave too?"

Riley grinned. "The only way Colin and Judy are leaving is when they're dead and ready to be buried."

"You've got that right," Colin said from the doorway. "No one and no thing is chasing us off our land. Not that mob next door, not our kids telling us we're getting too old and certainly not demons."

The word rang in her mind and she closed her eyes, trying to convince herself the moment wasn't real. Who believed in demons? When Riley took both her hands, she opened her eyes to see his concerned look. "Demons aren't real." She kept her voice low. Too low for Colin to hear her words.

"Judy said to tell you to wash up. Dinner is going out." Colin strode away before either of them could speak, his footsteps loud in the silence.

Aura continued to meet Riley's gaze. "Demons aren't real."

"Do you want to call your mum and tell her you're staying here tonight?"

"Will you stop doing that?" She jerked her hands out of his grip, once more glaring at him.

"You'll have to be a little more specific if you want me to know what you're talking about, sweetheart."

"And stop calling me that." She continued to glare at him, not impressed when he grinned. "Stop avoiding my questions."

"Most people don't appreciate the answers I give."

"Tell me exactly what is going on. And stop looking at me like that."

Riley chuckled. "Like what?"

"Like I'm the crazy one."

"Are you saying it's me who's the crazy one?" Riley continued to grin.

She stood up, forcing him to move away. "If you can't give me any answers, I'm going."

Riley captured her hand, drawing her back to him. "Demons are real and my family have been hunting them for generations."

"Hunter." She remembered his earlier comment about his name. 'It actually tells you more than you realise.'

Riley nodded, then gestured towards the vintage

phone. "Call your mum. The number for Blue Sky is on a scrap of paper underneath it."

"I'm not going to leave her over there. Not if she's in danger."

"If we try and get her out of there tonight, she could end up in more danger than she's in at the moment. As long as Curtis thinks she knows nothing, she should be safe. He's not about to do anything to her until he figures out if she'll be more useful to them alive."

"That won't take him long. Mum has no sense of self-preservation. She'll tell him anything he wants to know."

"He won't trust that she's telling the truth. He thinks everyone is as devious as him."

Once more she closed her eyes, wishing it was a nightmare that would vanish in the time it took to open her eyes. It didn't work. Riley remained in front of her, his warm brown eyes filled with concern. "Promise me nothing will happen to her."

"I can't. All I can promise is that I'm working on dealing with what is happening next door. Permanently."

"Permanently?"

Riley nodded, turning away to sift through the photos. "Curtis."

She stared down at the ones he'd set out in a line. Her mouth opened slightly, a sound escaping when she realised each photo was of the same man, spanning over a century judging by the other things and the fashions in the photos. Yet in each image the man remained the same. Impossibly ageless. "That's… that…" She swallowed hard. "That's impossible."

"He's not a demon."

"He's…" That hadn't occurred to her. She shook her head. "What is he?"

"Someone who has meddled in things, he shouldn't, for far too long."

"What sort of things?" When he didn't answer, she dragged her gaze from the images to look into Riley's eyes. "Riley?"

"Ritualistic slaughter of animals is only the start."

The many horror movies she'd watched over the years ran through her mind and she found herself asking the question she didn't really want the answer to, her voice whisper quiet. "What is the next step? What do they progress to after slaughtering animals?"

Footsteps sounded in the hallway. "Dinner is going cold. Judy will be annoyed if you don't hurry up." Colin remained there a moment before returning the way he'd come.

Aura barely spared Colin a glance, her gaze returning to Riley. She decided she wanted to know after all. Her mum and aunt were next door. She wasn't about to let anything happen to them. "What is their next step?" This time her voice was firm, her tone sharp.

"Human sacrifice."

She spun from him, striding towards the front door. "I'm getting them out of there."

Riley grabbed her arm, tugging her back from the screen. "No. Don't do anything stupid. Do you want to get the three of you killed?"

Jerking out of his grip, she met his gaze. "Do you expect me to leave them there to be sacrificed?" The photos came to mind, the animals quickly replaced by images of her mum and aunt.

"I've already told you he'll want to learn everything about Hazel first. She's safe for tonight."

"What about my aunt? Is she safe?"

Riley remained silent, compassion filling his gaze.

Fear flared and she backed away from him. "Aunt Zinnia isn't dead."

"I didn't say she was."

"But you looked like you had bad news to tell me."

"Do you have any other family?"

Aura shook her head.

"Then the best thing you can do for them is to stay here. As long as someone knows they're at Blue Sky, they're less likely to become the next sacrifice. They won't want to draw unnecessary attention."

His words had her swaying on her feet. "Next." The word was almost a squeak, the images of the slaughtered cows again returning to her.

"Aura." His voice was soft, his hands steadying her. "My family are trying to find out more information about Curtis. We won't allow him to escape. Nor will I let you do anything to warn him we're coming after him."

"Won't Feud warn him?"

"I'm the only demon hunter in the area. No threat as far as they're concerned."

"When will the rest of the hunters arrive?"

Riley chuckled. "I won't need to call on all the hunters. Besides, not all of them live in this country."

His earlier words came back to her. "Europe. Your parents are hunting demons in Europe?"

"Yeah." He gestured to the phone. "Ring your mum so we can have dinner. Judy is going to be really unimpressed with how long we're taking."

She was torn between ringing and leaving. Of trying to convince her family to head back to Brisbane with her. But convincing her mum of anything sensible was impossible. Moving to the desk, she lifted the heavy phone, finding the scrap of paper with the number of Blue Sky Community on top of many such scraps. She stared at the cursive writing before lifting the handle. The cord of the phone was twisted and kept getting in the way. It took far too long to dial the number, waiting for the rotary dial to return to the start before she could dial each digit.

"Blue Sky Community. How may I help you?"

Chapter Five

For a moment Aura couldn't speak, startled by the friendly sounding woman on the other end of the line. "Ah, I was wanting to speak to my mum. Hazel Redding. She's visiting her sister-"

"Oh, yes. I know Hazel. Such a lovely woman. You're so lucky to have a mum like her."

"Ah, yeah."

"Are you joining us for dinner? We're serving it in about twenty minutes."

For a second she began to wonder if Riley was wrong. How could the friendly woman she was talking to have anything to do with the photos on the coffee table? "Can I talk to my mum?"

"Of course you can." The woman laughed, a brittle, fake sound. "She's barely left her sister's side."

Aura gritted her teeth against the constant chatter. "I can talk to her now?"

The woman laughed once more. "I'm looking for them right now. The phone is cordless. A few of our community are sitting outside watching the stars. It's such a lovely night we were thinking of having a sing along. You should join us. Your mum said you have a beautiful singing voice."

Fear raced through her at the thought of her mum outside. "Is that safe?"

Riley shook his head, frowning at her.

"Is what safe?" the woman asked.

"I mean, we're out in the middle of nowhere. Isn't there dangerous wildlife out at night?"

The woman laughed again. "You are such a city child. Don't worry. Give it a couple of weeks and we'll soon teach you to love the country."

"A couple of weeks?" What had her mum agreed to?

"Here you go. I've found your mum." The woman's voice became muffled, but clear enough to be faintly heard. "Hazel, it's your daughter. You should tell her to join us for dinner and our evening entertainment. I'm sure she'd enjoy herself."

"Aura."

She leaned against the edge of the desk at the sound of her mum's voice, relieved to finally hear her. "You're okay?"

"Zinnia and I are having a marvellous time catching up. This place is amazing. I haven't seen her this relaxed in years. You should join us for dinner and the evening's entertainment."

There seemed to be a brightness to her mum's voice that it didn't typically hold. A fake brightness. "I was thinking of staying here the night. Riley invited me to dinner."

"And to think you were worried about not having anything to do while you're here."

This time her mum sounded like herself and Aura started to argue that it hadn't been lack of things to do that she'd complained about. It had been being kept busy running around cleaning up after her mum and having no time for herself. It looked like she'd been right to worry. As always, she didn't bother saying the words. "I'll join you in the morning."

Hazel giggled. "Finally. I thought a handsome guy would never catch your attention. Those plain ones you've dated over the years weren't right for you. They faded into the background. You should see some of the men here. Although many of them have odd names like Feud, Bane and Mayhem."

She started to argue that falling for a handsome face had always been one of her mum's biggest problems. Until Hazel spoke the names. For a moment she couldn't speak, her gaze colliding with Riley's "Feud?"

"Yes, such an odd name. And he's so tall."

Riley kept his voice low. "Don't say anything. She's safe as long as she doesn't know."

She closed her eyes against the worry she could see in Riley's eyes. "I'll see you in the morning, Mum. Dinner is ready." Her jaw tightened on all the warnings she wanted to give. Warnings she knew her mum would brush aside and ignore as always.

"Have fun, Aura."

"Yeah. You too." She nearly told her mum to be careful and that she loved her, but she didn't want to do anything out of the ordinary.

Hazel giggled. "Oh I'm planning to have a lot of fun."

Aura continued to hold the handset to her ear, even after her mum had hung up, opening her eyes when Riley took hold of her hand, squeezing lightly. She placed the handset in the cradle. "I can't leave her there."

"We can't get near Curtis. If you can convince your family to go on a picnic with you, I can help you break his hold over them. Whatever you do, you can't go over there. You'll end up under his influence too."

"You can break his hold?" Her initial hope faded. Likely her mum was there because of her own flaws, not because of some man who'd had too many dealings with demons. "It probably won't make a difference."

"What about for Zinnia?"

"Isn't anyone interested in eating? All that good food going to waste," Judy demanded from the doorway.

Riley grinned, drawing Aura forward. "I'm starving. We had to let Aura's family know where she is so they don't worry."

Judy led the way down the hallway to the kitchen at the other end. "She's not the one they should be worrying about. If they're next door they should be more worried about themselves."

Colin sat at a timber table, an ironed tablecloth angled to cover most of the surface except each corner. The edges of the white cloth were decorated by cutwork embroidery, solid cutlery at each place along with an upturned glass, a jug of water in the middle. "About time. She wouldn't dish up until you joined us." He glared at them.

Once Aura had washed her hands at the sink, she sat in the seat Judy motioned her to. "Sorry we took so long." She wanted to talk to Riley about Zinnia.

Was this why her aunt was acting out of character? But she didn't feel comfortable discussing the matter with Colin glaring at her from the head of the table.

She looked around the kitchen while Judy served the food, having shooed Riley to the table when he'd offered to help. The kitchen benches were solid timber, the painted doors faded and chipped, the varnished surrounds looking equally worn. Lace curtains hung at the windows, nothing visible outside in the darkness. The floor was scuffed, polished timber and a garish coloured bathroom could be seen through an open door. The tub and vanity were a matching pink that had lost none of their brightness or if they had, she hated to think how bright they'd once been.

Judy set a plate of roast vegetables and sliced beef drowned in gravy in front of Aura, reaching across the table to place a full plate in front of Riley. She returned a moment later with two more plates, setting one in front of Colin. Once she was seated, she looked towards Riley.

Aura was about to ask what they were waiting for when Riley bowed his head and said Grace. She stared at him, having never before met someone who gave thanks for their food. A glance at Colin showed he wasn't impressed, his glare increasing until Riley finished and he was able to eat. Aura didn't immediately eat, her gaze on Riley as she studied him. When he looked up from his meal, he grinned.

"Aren't you hungry?" Judy gestured towards Aura's plate. "You're not on a diet are you?"

"No. I mean yes. I mean-" She broke off, taking a deep breath before she answered Judy's questions. "I'm not on a diet and I am hungry."

"You're not one of them vegetarians are you?" Colin demanded, making the word sound like it was a contagious disease.

When Aura caught sight of the humour in Riley's eyes, she nearly laughed. In an effort not to offend the elderly man, she shook her head and had a mouthful of food, making sure to have some of the beef too.

Colin grunted as if he wasn't sure she was telling the truth, returning his attention to his dinner.

Swallowing her food, Aura said to Riley, "I thought demons were meant to be powerful."

"There are rules they have to abide by."

"What sort of rules? Why can't they throw Colin and Judy off their land?" She glanced at each of them. "No offence to either of you, but you have to admit that Feud was massive. And strong looking."

"He can't come in here," Colin said.

"Why not? What's stopping him?" Aura asked Colin.

Colin pointed towards Riley with his fork. "Him."

Aura turned to Riley, who spoke before she could ask him what Colin meant.

"I'm not the one who's stopping demons from entering the house. Emily sent a priest out here. He arrived early this morning to bless the house and hopefully left before any of them realised he'd visited."

"Bless the house?" Her food remained barely touched. "Like in a horror movie?"

Riley chuckled, nodding to her food. "I thought you were hungry."

She was, but she wanted answers more. She had a mouthful of food and waited until she'd finished it before she spoke again. "How are you going to stop Curtis?"

"That's what I'd like to know." Colin picked up the jug, pouring himself and Judy a glass of water.

"Feud changes things a bit. A demon willing to serve as long as necessary and call on other demons is a problem. I might have to lead him away from here and let another hunter take over. He should follow me since he has a personal grudge."

"Don't want the place crawling with strangers,"

Colin grumbled. He pointed his fork at Riley again. "You I said could stay. Not a lot of others."

"What about Emily and Dan? They could take over here while I lead Feud away," Riley said.

Colin shrugged, eating more of his meal.

"How would you lead him away?" Aura nearly smiled when Riley glanced at her food. She'd been eating while they'd been talking. "How do demons usually track people down?"

"Blood."

She'd been about to have another mouthful, but lowered her fork, the images from earlier filling her mind. Her appetite fled and she swallowed hurriedly, trying to ignore the way her stomach turned. "That's how he found you this time?"

Riley shook his head. "I doubt it. Another demon probably told him I was here. They talk amongst themselves and share information in exchange for something. Often for power."

"How can you make sure he'll know where you go if you leave? Do you need to leave a blood trail or something?"

Judy frowned. "I really don't think this is the right kind of subject to be discussing at the dinner table."

"Sorry." Aura stared down at her food. Judy was probably correct. She should have eaten first. She ran the fork through the gravy, not sure she could manage another bite.

"Cows arrived safely," Colin said abruptly.

Judy slowly shook her head. "Seems a waste paying someone to agist our own cattle when we have all those acres full of feed."

Aura listened to Colin ramble on about costs and selling the cows once the market was right and holding off on getting more cattle until Curtis and his lot were gone. She slowly pieced part of the situation together from what he was saying. None of it looked good. When Judy rose to her feet, her food eaten, Aura was surprised to realise she'd automatically begun eating while she'd listened to the conversation.

Judy put her plate beside the sink, along with her glass. "I'll be in my bedroom if you need me. Answering a letter one of my sons sent. Every time they write they complain we don't have email. There's nothing wrong with putting pen to paper every once in a while." Judy walked to the start of the hallway as she spoke, looking over her shoulder as she paused there. "My bedroom is across from the lounge room if you need anything. You can stay in the room Emily used while she was here. I put fresh linen on the bed yesterday."

Colin rose from the table as his wife walked down

the hallway. He glared at them again. "Don't go expecting me to wash all the extra dishes having the two of you here has created."

Riley chuckled as Colin also left the kitchen. "Guess we're on clean up duty." He rose from the table. "Any preference? Washing or drying?"

"Either." She helped herself to a drink of water, checking they were alone before she spoke. "How do you get Feud to follow you?"

"That will be difficult. I can't exactly give him my blood without him, or Curtis, expecting an ulterior motive."

"You'd have to-" She broke off, wishing once again that she hadn't eaten dinner.

Riley gathered the dishes, heading to the sink. "It's how demons track people." He turned on the tap. "Amongst other things."

It took her a moment before she could join him at the sink, bringing the glasses. "A blessed house won't stop humans from entering. What will you do if Curtis comes over here and tries to deal with Colin and Judy himself?"

"If he's had as many dealings with demons as I suspect he has, then he probably won't be able to enter the house. Or at least not easily." Riley rinsed off the dishes.

"How do you know demons aren't outside waiting for you to go out there?"

Riley held out his hand, showing the lines that wrapped around his left wrist. "Demon mark. I can tell if there are any nearby. There are some major ones at a distance."

"Demon mark? I thought it was a tattoo." She collected the tea towel that hung on the front of the oven.

"Most people do." He put the washed cutlery in the draining rack. "You seem pretty calm for someone who's learned about the existence of demons."

She shrugged. "I'm probably becoming immune to the many disasters my mum gets herself involved in." She shrugged again. "I still haven't figured out if this one is worse than living with a murderer for a month."

"You lived with a murderer? How did that happen? Who was the one who figured out they were a murderer?"

Chapter Six

A wry smile formed as she took the plate he'd put in the draining rack. "He had nice blue eyes. Or at least he did according to Mum. To this day Mum thinks the police were mistaken and eventually he'll be released and the real murderer found. Not that she probably thinks about it much. If at all." She met his gaze, surprised by the compassion she could see in his warm, brown eyes. "His first kill was an accident. We were going to be his first planned kill, the ones who made him more than a murderer. We would have helped him become a serial killer."

"Trust me, this is worse. Demons aren't something you want to mess with. The police aren't going to cart them away and lock them up. As long as someone keeps summoning them, they can keep coming after you."

"How will you stop Feud?"

"That's a really good question." Putting the last of the dishes in the draining rack, Riley pulled the plug.

She stared at him as the water gurgled down the drain. "You don't know how to stop him? I thought you said you're a demon hunter."

Riley grinned. "That doesn't mean I have all the answers." He took the tea towel from her and dried the rest of the dishes.

"What did you mean earlier about helping me break Curtis' hold over my family? What sort of hold would he have on them?"

"The sort of hold where they have lost part of their will to make their own choices."

"Aunt Zinnia." The woman was strong willed and sensible, not the type of person who'd sell up and move to a commune, constantly encouraging her younger sister to join her. "She hasn't been herself for months."

"I can help you get her back. But you need to make sure it doesn't interfere with bringing Curtis down," Riley warned.

"Okay. What do I need to do?"

"That's it? No other questions?"

She smiled at the surprise she heard in his voice. "I've gone into situations with less information and not having a clue how to rescue Mum." She shrugged. "This is rather organised by comparison."

"You have no siblings?"

"No. You?"

"Yeah. A brother. Blake." He took hold of her hand, holding it firmly. "He'd be here within hours if I needed him. So would many others. We aren't alone even though it would appear that way."

"You're lucky." There'd been a few times she'd thought a sibling would have been nice. Someone to share the burden with. But knowing her luck, she would have had two to look after.

"Yeah, I am." He glanced at the doorway. "Did you want me to show you to your room?"

"What I'd love is a shower after how hot today has been. A pity all my gear is in Mum's car."

"I can lend you a t-shirt. It'd probably come to mid thigh." He looked her up and down, grinning. "Not sure how well my boxers would stay up." He paused a moment, his grin becoming wider. "And I don't think you'd like to borrow something from Judy. The last time she bought any clothes would have been about thirty years ago."

"T-shirt and boxers it is." Anything had to be better than the sweaty clothes she wore.

"Wait here."

He hurried off before she could tell him she didn't want to be left alone. Had the flicker she'd seen in Feud's eyes been fire and not a reflection of the headlights like she'd thought? She slowly crossed the kitchen and stood at the back door, the timber door open, the screen keeping insects out. Everything was dark. Not even the moon could be seen from where she stood, the stars doing very little to help with how the night blanketed the land.

"Here you go."

She spun to face Riley, heart racing, not having heard him enter the kitchen. Her gaze brushed over the towel and clothes he held before she looked into his eyes. "I didn't realise how dark it would be out there."

"Nothing like the city. Or a town."

She took the clothes from him, frowning at the silver safety pin he held out. "What's that for?"

"Judy gave it to me along with the towel when I said you were borrowing some of my clothes to have a shower. Said you might need it to hold up the boxers."

"Oh. Thanks." She took a step towards the bathroom. "Why are you helping me?"

"I'm a hunter. It's my job."

"You get paid for doing this?"

He chuckled. "You could say that." He nodded towards the bathroom. "Once you're finished in there your bedroom is the first one on the right and mine is on the left."

"Okay." She remained where she was, feeling awkward. "Thanks." She nodded towards the bathroom. "I'll…"

Riley nodded before striding from the kitchen.

She watched him enter the first room on the left in the shadowy hallway, closing the door behind him. Looking further along the hallway, she realised the light at the far end near the door was turned off. For some reason that made her uneasy. Logically she knew lights wouldn't be left on all night, but it bothered her. Rather than dwell on it, she hurried into the bathroom, closing and locking the door behind her.

The silence in the bathroom made her feel alone. Like she was the star of a horror film. She eyed the plastic shower curtain that hung on the rod that was spotted with rust. It was half closed. Reaching out as far as possible, she took a small step forward to slide it across, bunching it up to one side. The bathtub was empty. No knife-wielding maniacs were hiding behind the curtain. Yet her heart continued to race and she kept feeling like something was about to happen.

Why couldn't she have had a highly organised and sensible mother? One who worked a regular job and had a savings account. Stripping off, she hurriedly showered, drying and dressing herself in record time. It was a relief to leave the bathroom, taking her bundle of sweaty clothes with her. She'd needed to use the safety pin Judy had provided. The silence in the bathroom, after the initial clang of the pipes from the water coming through them, had been unnerving.

Stopping in the doorway of the room Judy had said she could use, she glanced around. A timber duchess was off to her right, dainty crystal containers arranged on the lace doilies. A double bed was to her left, the chenille bedspread looking threadbare and doing nothing to hide the many lumps in the mattress. About the only comfort the room appeared to have was a thick oval rug at the side of the bed covering the timber floorboards and long curtains hiding the darkness outside.

She took her phone from the pocket of her jeans before leaving the bundle of clothes and her sneakers on the floor to the right of the door. Checking the time she was surprised to find it was nearly eight-thirty. Although she supposed she shouldn't be surprised since the sun set later at this time of year. With March approaching that'd change and the days would become shorter and cool off. Placing her phone on the duchess she once more looked around the room. Not wanting to remain by herself any longer, she crossed the hallway to knock softly on Riley's door. The sound of a television drifted down the hallway from the lounge room. If that was where Colin had gone she certainly didn't want to go in there to face any more of his glares.

The bedroom door opened. Riley didn't speak immediately. "You okay?"

"It's quiet." When he grinned, she added, "Too quiet." When he looked her up and down she had the urge to tug the t-shirt down lower.

He opened the door wider and stepped back. "I was checking supplies." He gestured to the duchess on her left. It was identical to the one in her room. There was a mixture of weapons scattered across it as well as several vials and an unlabelled water bottle filled with a clear liquid.

She gestured to the bottle as she entered the bedroom, noticing the sword he'd left by the front door was on the floor next to the double bed. "What's that?"

"Holy water."

"Is that what you threw at Feud earlier?"

"Yeah."

Picking up one of the vials, she examined it. "Is this holy water too?"

He held out a second vial. "Keep them. They won't stop a demon, but they might slow one down long enough to give you time to escape."

"How do you stop one?"

"Very few can be stopped permanently." He picked up a cross on a leather necklace, holding it out to her.

She glanced at the two daggers next to a quiver of arrows, the crystal containers pushed to the back of the duchess and the doilies looking out of place beneath the weapons. "I'd rather have them."

He chuckled. "Why doesn't that surprise me? Have you used a dagger before?"

"One of Mum's boyfriends taught me to throw daggers. He used to be in a circus." She grinned at his startled expression. "Nothing about my life has been conventional."

He took a step closer, slipping the leather necklace over her head and lifting her hair out of the way before he slid the leather knots along the leather to shorten the necklace. "Can you use a bow?"

"No. At least not as well as I can use throwing daggers."

He stepped back. "A sword?"

"Not really. But I can joust."

Laughter burst from Riley. "Well that wasn't something I would have expected."

She shrugged. "Mum has always been drawn to strange or unconventional people."

"That sounds like an understatement." Riley tugged a suitcase out from under the bed, lifting the lid to reveal more weapons and a handful of clothes. He chose two daggers before standing and offering them to her, hilt first.

She looked between the daggers and the weapons in his suitcase. "You travel with all this?"

"Sometimes." He continued to hold out the daggers.

"And you think other people are strange." She took the daggers, checking the weight and balance. "How do people who aren't hunters tell the difference between demons and humans?" She glanced at the demon mark on his wrist. "When they don't have one of those warning things."

"Demon marks are gained from dealing with demons. You get too involved and you will end up with one."

She stared at his wrist, not sure if that was good or bad.

"Is your hair a natural colour?"

"Yes. Why?" She met his gaze, trying to figure out why he'd ask such an odd question.

"Get too close to a demon, in dealing with them, and dyed hair and tattoos can end up blood red."

She thought of the small tattoo her mother had, a butterfly on her ankle. The outline had been done in blue with a light wash of colour across the wings. "What about if someone is under Curtis' control. Will that change the colour of a tattoo?"

"No. At least it shouldn't. But who knows exactly what he's doing over there."

"Shouldn't you know?"

"I can't step on his property without being surrounded by minor demons during the day and major ones of a night. I need to work on getting rid of the demons so I can get close to him. And get rid of them in a way that won't have him trying to escape."

She heard the sound of heavy footsteps, in the hallway, passing the room. She glanced at the closed door.

"Colin will be getting ready for bed. He goes to sleep every night around nine. Then he's up with the sun."

"It must be nice knowing what to expect each day."

"Is it?"

"Why wouldn't it be?"

"Imagine the most ordinary day you have ever experienced."

It took her a moment since there were so few of them. "Okay. Got it."

"Now repeat it. Thousands of times. Imagine reliving it every day."

Over and over it replayed in her mind, the details becoming clearer each time.

"That is your life as a vet." His voice was soft.

Shock arrowed through her and she took an involuntary step back, freezing before she retreated further. Her gaze narrowed. "No. You're wrong."

"Am I?"

"Stop messing with my head."

"Add a few unexpected things into those days. Aim for a little balance. That's all you're lacking."

She backed away from him. "No. You have no idea. You haven't lived my life." She felt the handle of the door press into her back, halting her. Behind the door she heard Colin's heavy footsteps as he headed towards his bedroom.

"What if you hadn't lived your life?" He gestured towards the daggers. "Learned unusual skills, met unique people." He held her gaze. "How would you have reacted when you learned that demons existed?"

She opened her mouth to argue his words, but had no idea what to say. "Goodnight." She glanced at the daggers. "Thanks." Turning, she opened the door.

"Don't go outside in the morning. Minor demons can walk about in the day."

Keeping her back to him, she tried not to be bothered by his words. But she was. How was she to leave if there were demons outside waiting for her? "Okay." She closed the door behind her, glancing up and down the hallway. Each end was in darkness, only the lights in her room and Riley's casting any light into the hallway, the decorative panel above the doors lit up from behind. She moved closer to her room, unable to bring herself to peer into the darkness again.

Chapter Seven

Closing her door, Aura set the daggers and vials of holy water on the floor beside the bed before turning back the linen. She looked from the bed to the light switch several times before she decided there was no way she'd manage to sleep if she put the light out. Climbing into bed she tried not to think about her mum. Riley better be right and her mum survived the night. A hollow feeling filled her at the thought of losing her mum. It was quickly replaced by a rush of anger and determination. That wasn't going to happen. Tomorrow she was getting the lot of them out of here. They'd return to Brisbane and forget all about this latest episode.

The flickers of light she'd seen in Feud's eyes came back to her, followed by the images of the photos. If she managed to sleep at all it'd be a miracle. And an even larger miracle if she didn't have a nightmare.

Riley's words came back to her. He was wrong. She didn't want an unusual life. It had been forced on her. Images from her life flickered through her mind, interrupted by the photos, including the ones of Curtis. Surely she'd still be herself if she'd grown up in a stable environment. He had to be wrong.

An image of Riley's warm, brown eyes filled her mind, overpowering the images of the ritualistic slaughters. An unsettled feeling grew as she replayed her most ordinary day. She wouldn't want to relive that a thousand times. Yet neither did she want to worry every day about how she'd feed herself or afford rent.

Balance. She worried at the word like she'd worried at loose teeth when she'd been younger. Gently probing until she was more certain of it. Balance. She'd never considered that before. Again the images of the slaughtered livestock came to mind and she shuddered. She needed to figure out a new plan. There was no way she could be a vet. Or anything else that involved blood.

It took her ages to fall asleep. The light and the images made it difficult, along with the lumpy mattress. She was woken far too early the next morning by the sound of heavy footsteps passing her room. For a moment she laid there, disorientated.

The night before descended on her in a rush and she swallowed hard as she tried to push away the images of the slaughtered livestock.

It had to have been Colin passing her room. Riley was more silent than that. She stared at the closed door, not really sure she wanted to face Colin yet. In the end, she needed to use the bathroom. Leaving the light on, she made her way to the kitchen, relieved to find Judy was also awake. "Morning."

"Noticed you didn't say it was good," Colin muttered.

Judy looked over her shoulder with a smile. "Morning, love. Tea or coffee?"

"Ah, coffee I guess." When neither of them spoke again, she retreated to the bathroom. Coming back out, she paused in the doorway, spotting Riley coming in the back door. He wore a black t-shirt today with his black jeans. "You were outside?" She instantly realised how lame the question was. "I mean, there are no demons out there?"

"Two minor ones. They left me alone while I took the motorbike off the ute so I decided I'd wait until I've had breakfast to get rid of them." Riley took the coffee cup Judy handed him, smiling at her in thanks. He faced Aura again. "A couple of arrows doused in holy water and a few prayers should send them home."

Aura took a coffee cup from Judy with a smile and a soft 'thanks'. "Home?"

"Hell of course," Colin stated.

She started to comment on his tone, then decided it wasn't worth the grief. As soon as she had her family, they were getting out of here. "After that, can-"

Riley cut her off. "Let's not give anything away." He glanced at the window.

She moved closer so she could see through it. The colour of dawn filled the sky, but that wasn't what held her gaze. It was the man standing near a hills hoist clothesline that caught her attention. He looked ordinary other than the ripple of colours that moved across his skin. Browns and greenish browns. "Is that-" She gestured towards the figure, unable to finish the question.

"One of them." Riley dropped bread into the toaster.

She looked at Judy, Colin and Riley. None of them seemed bothered by the demon outside the kitchen window. "You're going to wait until after breakfast?"

Riley leaned against the kitchen bench, grinning at her. "Yep. I don't think they'll mind."

Colin chuckled. "I think the minding will come

when you go out there with your arrows and holy water."

The toast popped and Aura jumped slightly. Were they all mad? Demons were outside the house and they were making breakfast and joking.

Riley dropped the toast on a plate. "Did you want any toast?"

She stared at him. "Are you serious?"

His grin remained in place. "Ask my family. They'll tell you I'm rarely serious."

She opened her mouth several times before she spun and started to stride from the kitchen.

"If you want me to wash your clothes they'll be ready in a couple of hours," Judy called out. "With the heat already building it won't take more than an hour for them to dry. Once I get them on the line."

"Enough time for me to deal with other things," Riley said.

She looked over her shoulder, not sure what she should do. The thought of wearing her sweaty clothes made the decision easy. "I'll bring them out." As she returned to her room, she heard Riley speaking.

"Now don't you go thinking you can go outside to the laundry on your own, Judy. You make sure you wait for me to go out there with you."

She didn't know if Judy spoke too quietly for her to hear or the woman remained silent. Gathering her clothes she returned to the kitchen to find a cane basket of dirty clothes sitting beside the back door. She dropped her clothes in it when Judy nodded at her enquiring look.

Not knowing what else to do, and feeling hungry, she made toast, smearing jam across it when it was done. It seemed odd sitting around eating breakfast while a demon remained outside. Her gaze was frequently drawn to the window. Eventually she couldn't help asking, "Should we be concerned." She nodded in the direction of the demon.

"I guess that depends on what you want to do."

Saying that she didn't want to stay here any longer wouldn't be polite. So she remained silent.

Judy headed for the back door. "Day is marching on."

"Let me get that for you." Riley picked up the basket before Judy could, leading the way.

Aura glanced at Colin, hoping he didn't expect her to talk to him as she had no idea what to say. What did you talk about when a demon stood metres away, listening to every word spoken. Finishing her toast, she washed her hands and rinsed off her plate, stacking it beside the sink. Another glance at the demon had her wandering towards the back door. She saw no one out there. Next she checked out her bedroom window. The area was clear. She glanced at Riley's closed door as she headed towards the front of the house. Hesitating, she remained at the screen door, peering through it. After a couple of seconds she stepped onto the verandah, closing the door quietly behind her.

Spotting the demon off to her left, she froze. It was staring directly at her, piercing dark eyes with the flicker of flames in their depths. She couldn't drag her gaze from him. He was more ordinary looking than the one out the back. His dusky skin was a single colour, his features looked human and his body wasn't an unusual height.

"What are you doing out there?"

Her heart thudded in her chest as she turned to face Riley. "Quit sneaking up on me."

Riley opened the door and stepped back for her to enter. "I was going to collect my bow and arrows when I saw you outside."

"Can I help?"

"Do you know any prayers?"

"The Lord's Prayer."

"Really?"

A smile slowly formed at hearing the surprise in

Riley's voice. It seemed so little surprised him. "A group of people Mum hung out with one year loved theological debates. They must have dissected that prayer so many times that I ended up learning it off by heart."

"Perfect." He returned her smile. "Once I shoot, you start praying. That'll make the holy water burn. With both of us praying it will send them home quicker."

She glanced down at her clothes. At least she wouldn't need to fight. Not something she wanted to do in her borrowed clothes. "Okay. I can manage that." Not that it sounded like she'd be much help. It reminded her of the unnecessary jobs she often gave her mum to keep her out of the way. While he was in his bedroom, she collected the daggers and vials of holy water, wanting to be armed when they faced the demons. She was coming out of her room when a thought occurred to her. She hurried after Riley who was returning to the front door, bow in hand, quiver of arrows on his belt. "Will they attack together?"

"Let's pray they don't."

"That doesn't sound like a good plan."

Riley chuckled. "It's actually a better plan than you might think." He opened the screen door, ushering her through before he closed it. "Remember to pray once I shoot him, sweetheart."

She glared at him. "Was that deliberate?"

He nocked an arrow, drawing it back. "Was what deliberate?"

She had no idea what to do with all that she held so she placed a vial and dagger on the floor at her feet, keeping a vial in her left hand and a throwing dagger in her right. "My name is Aura."

Riley let loose the arrow, glancing at her. "I know. Sweetheart."

Gritting her teeth she began to recite the prayer, Riley's voice echoing hers. The demon roared, striding towards them. Faltering, she took a step back. Did a blessed house keep all demons out?

"Keep going." Riley had a second arrow ready, rejoining her in praying as he fired.

The demon roared once more, staggering.

She wanted to tell him it didn't seem to be working, the demon continued to stride towards them, but she didn't dare stop praying. Her grip tightened on the vial of holy water as the demon reached the bottom of the stairs. A touch of relief raced through her when the demon was unable to come any closer.

Riley kept firing arrows at the demon, his voice

strong as he recited the prayer with her. The demon vanished, arrows falling to the ground, and still Riley continued to the end of the prayer.

Not knowing if it was important to keep going, she followed his lead, waiting until it was done to speak. "Why did you keep praying once the demon was gone?" It seemed like an unimportant question considering they'd faced a demon. What she really should have been asking him was why he didn't get a safer job. She doubted it was usually this easy to deal with demons. She thought of the one out the back. Not long and she could work on rescuing her mum and aunt.

"It's always good to finish a prayer." Riley gathered the arrows then nodded in the direction of the door. "Ready to deal with the second one?" He rejoined her on the verandah.

"Sure." The blessed house should make dealing with the second demon a breeze. "Then we can..." She tried to think of a way to mention their plans without letting the remaining demon know.

Riley nodded. "Yep." He strode along the hallway.

She gathered the other dagger and vial before she followed him through the house, remaining on the back steps with him. "Can the demon get us here?" She glanced around the area, frowning. "Where is it?"

"It can't get us here, but the problem is, neither can we get it." Riley gestured to the laundry, a small building that jutted out from the back of the house, blocking the view of the hills hoist. "He's behind there." Riley stepped onto the grass.

Aura remained where she was.

"You don't have to help," Riley said. "I can take care of him."

She moved to the lowest step. "Would praying from here help?"

"It's okay. I've been fighting demons for years."

She looked into his eyes, seeing the reassurance in them. It made her feel worse. "I'll help." She never let anyone fight her battles for her. Taking a deep breath, she joined him on the grass. It felt dry beneath her bare feet, the morning dew long gone in the already warm morning.

"They can move quick. Stay behind me and don't stop praying."

She wished she wore her jeans so she could tuck the vials into a pocket. Not knowing what else to do with them, she lifted the hem of the t-shirt and tucked them into the waistband of the boxers so she could have a dagger in each hand. She'd rather lose the holy water than the daggers. "Okay." She followed well behind him, scanning the area as they walked around the laundry. It wasn't until they were nearly on the other side of the laundry that she spotted the demon, his motley skin blending with the tree behind the building, wide spreading branches creating plenty of shade. The hills hoist was between the laundry and the tree.

Riley raised his bow. "What name do you currently go by, demon?"

"Havoc." The demon nodded to the arrow pointed at him. "Is that supposed to make me fear you?"

"Return to where you came from or we'll return you there, Havoc," Riley said.

The demon chuckled. "Think that will keep me from returning? Curtis has promised to call us back when we're banished."

Havoc's raspy voice sent shivers down her spine. How did Riley expect to stop Curtis when he could keep calling on demons to help?

Riley fired, his arrow sinking into the demon's chest. "Tell him I will keep sending you back for as long as he keeps summoning you."

Havoc roared, ripping the arrow from his flesh and tossing it on the ground. "Why not tell him yourself?" The demon strode towards Riley who backed away, firing again.

Aura also backed away, belatedly starting to pray,

having been shocked by how little the arrow had seemed to bother Havoc.

Instead of answering the demon, Riley joined Aura in her prayer, firing another arrow at him.

Once more Havoc roared, hissing as his gaze turned to Aura. "I will come after both of you when I return and make you feel every bit of the pain you are currently causing me. You will want an army at your back."

Riley fired again. "We don't need an army to face any of you. Including Curtis. In fact, I can manage to deal with all of you on my own." He fired again.

Havoc roared. "Fool." He launched himself past Riley and at Aura.

She stumbled back, the words of the prayer impossible to remember.

Before Havoc could reach Aura, Riley dropped his bow and barrelled into the demon, knocking him down, ending up on the ground with him. As they fought, arrows scattered across the grass from Riley's quiver.

Chapter Eight

Aura froze, her gaze fixed on Riley and Havoc. The sound of a gunshot had her spinning. Colin stood with his rifle pointed at the figures fighting on the ground. Fear was replaced by disgust. An elderly man was fighting back. What was wrong with her that she stood by watching? Raising her right hand, she aimed the dagger at the rolling figures, beginning to pray again. Colin fired and the sound of the rifle made her jump and her words falter. She momentarily closed her eyes, opening them to look for an opportunity. The moment she saw it, she threw the dagger, transferring the second dagger to her right hand as the demon howled. There was a slight burning sensation in her left wrist, but she didn't have time to see what insect had bitten her. She tightened her grip on the remaining dagger, looking for an opportunity to throw it.

Havoc tried to escape Riley who had a dagger in his hand. He drove it into the demon's chest and the creature vanished in a burst of light. Riley collapsed on the ground, rolling onto his back to stare up at Aura with a grin.

She took a step towards him, glancing around the area before moving closer. She couldn't see any demons. "Are you hurt?" His shirt and arms were smeared with a dark liquid.

Colin joined her. "Judy's going to be annoyed about you making more washing for her."

Riley chuckled, scrambling to his feet, gathering his bow and arrows and the dagger. "I'll rinse the demon blood off them before she washes them. Probably best not to find out what that would do to her washing machine." He faced Aura, his grin fading. "Are you okay?" He looked her up and down. "I know he didn't get to you, but-"

Remorse struck her. He might've been fighting demons for years, but she'd offered to help. "I didn't mean to stop praying."

He reached for her, lowering his hand when he glanced at the demon blood on himself. "You did well. I was surprised how well you managed considering you've never fought demons before." He grinned. "Been in a lot of fights have you?"

"Not really. Only a couple." She'd seen more than her fair share though at some of the places her mum had taken her.

"I'll return the dagger to you when it's clean." Riley glanced around the area. "We better make plans before more demons arrive." Another grin formed. "After I clean up though. I doubt Judy would be impressed with me sitting at her kitchen table covered in demon blood."

Aura walked between Riley and Colin, waiting in the kitchen with Colin and Judy, who was baking biscuits, while Riley showered. She stood awkwardly by the back door, not sure what she should do. The sound of running water could be clearly heard in the kitchen and Aura frequently glanced towards the closed door.

Colin reloaded his weapon, drawing back the bolt to slip several cartridges in before pushing the bolt back into place.

Aura sat at the table, placing the dagger and two vials of holy water in front of her. The tablecloth had been removed from the table and the worn timber was now visible. She put her hands in her lap when she noticed the tremble in them. She'd fought demons. Had actually thrown a dagger at something living. Or at least she assumed demons could be considered living creatures.

Colin rose to his feet, carrying the rifle. "Might go figure out what that boy did to my bike. After I throw a few more cartridges in my pockets." He ambled towards the front of the house.

Judy slowly shook her head as she slipped the two trays of biscuits into the oven. "That bike hasn't worked right since the day they brought it home. Wouldn't listen to me though. The boys were determined to have a bike and Colin was just as bad." She stopped by the table. "Do you need anything?"

"I'm okay." Or at least as okay as she was likely to be with her family next door and possibly under the influence of demons.

"Then I'll leave you to it. I have a cutwork bedspread I'm working on. You let me know if you need anything. I'll be sitting in the rocking chair in my bedroom. By the window. There's good light in there. No trees to block it."

Riley came out of the bathroom as Judy reached the start of the hallway. "I've left the clothes in the tub. I'll throw them in the clothes basket later when they dry out a bit."

Judy nodded, before continuing along the hallway.

Riley joined Aura at the table, holding out the throwing dagger. "Thanks for fighting with me."

She met his gaze, surprised by the approval she saw in his warm, brown eyes. "That's okay." She took the dagger, placing it on the table next to the other one.

Riley sat across from her. "Have you ever been on a picnic with your mum before?"

"Yeah. Lots of times." Images of running barefoot through long grass came to her, her mum carrying a colourful blanket over her shoulder, various people with them all carrying different food.

"There's a stream not far from here that runs past an old graveyard, which hasn't been used for decades. It's still hallowed though."

"What does that mean?"

"Consecrated."

"No, not the meaning. What does it mean for us?"

Riley grinned. "Demons can't step onto hallowed ground. Just like they can't enter blessed buildings."

"So demons won't be able to stop whatever we do to break Curtis' hold over them?"

"It would work like that if we planned to have the picnic in the graveyard. But no, it's to tell us if either of them are possessed. They won't be able to enter if a demon is in possession of their bodies."

Aura stared at Riley, mouth half open, a sick feeling

in the pit of her stomach. It took her several attempts before she could speak. "Possessed?" The word came out sounding nothing like her.

"It's okay. We'll deal with it if either of them are possessed. But we need to know so we can deal with it." He reached across the table, picking up one of the vials. "This is what will break Curtis' hold on them."

She stared at the vial. "Holy water." She didn't bother to keep the scepticism from her voice.

Riley chuckled. "Trust me." He rose to his feet. "Ring your mum and convince her to come on a picnic with you and bring your aunt. A family picnic. Tell them to meet you here at midday. That'll give us time to prepare everything."

"A family picnic? On my own?" What if one of them was possessed? She shook her head. "I can't-"

"I'll be there. But we don't want anyone else to join us. I'll meet you at the graveyard. I'll bring along a thermos of coffee that you've supposedly left behind."

She looked into his brown eyes, not sure if she should trust the assurances she saw in them. She'd never had to do anything like this before. The flicker of flames she'd seen in the dark eyes of the first demon she'd helped Riley banish came to mind. "What if you don't arrive in time?"

"I'll be there before you. Where no one will see

me." He paused a moment. "You don't have to do this, but it might be the only way to get your family to safety."

Clasping her hands in her lap, she tried to keep them from trembling. She didn't want anything to happen to her family. Her mum and aunt were all she had. No cousins, no grandparents and no father. They were it. "Okay."

Riley rose, pushing his chair back under the table. "When your mum picks you up, make sure you're the one who drives."

"Why?"

Riley walked towards the hallway, glancing at her when she didn't immediately join him. "You need to be the one in control of every step. Don't give the demons a chance to take over either through possession or through an order they've given your family."

"Okay." She trailed behind Riley, having left the daggers and vials on the table, noticing a spot of dirt on her left wrist. Rubbing at it, she realised it wasn't dirt. Before it could fully sink in that she had a demon mark, admittedly an extremely small one, Riley gestured towards the phone.

"Want me to stay with you or would you rather talk to your mum alone?"

She clasped her hands behind her back, not sure she wanted him to notice the demon mark he'd warned her she might gain. "Stay. I might have trouble convincing her."

Riley nodded, remaining by the desk.

She lifted up the phone for the number on the piece of paper underneath, returning it once she'd dialled. The call was answered immediately by the same friendly sounding woman from last night.

"Blue Sky Community. How may I help you?"

"Hi. Is my mum there? Hazel Redding."

"Aura. How lovely to talk to you again. Are you joining us today?"

"Yeah. Is Mum there?"

"Of course she is, dear. Where else would she be? She was so disappointed you didn't join us last night."

She tried not to let her annoyance at being called 'dear' enter her voice. Particularly since the woman's tone sounded more than a little patronising as she spoke the word. "Can I speak to my mum?"

"Did you want us to send a four-wheel-drive over for you? That driveway next door is dreadful, isn't it?"

"It's okay. I can meet mum out the front."

"Shall I pass that message along to her?"

Aura didn't answer immediately, not sure what she should say. She looked to Riley for inspiration.

"Ask if there is something wrong."

His voice was soft enough Aura could barely hear him. She nodded. "Is something wrong? Is there a reason I can't talk to my mum?"

The woman laughed. A brittle, fake sound. "Why would anything be wrong, dear?"

Aura's jaw tightened and she paused a moment before she spoke. "I don't know. You tell me. Dear."

Riley shook his head, a warning in his eyes.

"Here she is now. I'm sure she'll tell you how much she missed not having you here last night."

Aura listened to the slightly muffled directions the woman gave her mum, gritting her teeth, her hand tightening into a fist. She met Riley's gaze again when he took hold of her hand, uncurling her fingers.

He glanced at her hand, his gaze immediately focusing on the small mark on her left wrist. A grin formed and once more he met her gaze.

She drew her hand from his, turning her back on him, not sure what to think about the demon mark.

"Aura. I missed not having you here last night. I'll come and pick you up now. You'll meet me at the front gate."

Her mum's tone had her hand curling into a fist again. "Mum." Her voice broke and she started again.

"Remember those picnics we went on when I was younger."

Hazel chuckled. "How could I forget? You complained until we arrived then you'd run through the long grass chasing the puppy one of the girls always brought with her."

She'd forgotten about the puppy. It had been impossible to find in the long grass. Until it moved. "They were so much fun. The picnics."

"We should go on one again," Hazel said.

"Riley showed me a stream that reminded me of them." She met his gaze when he stepped in front of her. "We should have a family picnic. You, me and Aunt Zinnia. Just the three of us."

"That sounds lovely. We'll have to do that during our stay here."

"What about today?" Aura asked.

"You're coming here today."

A shiver ran through Aura at the tone of voice her mum used. She hadn't sounded in the least bit like herself. "I know. After a picnic though. The two of you can pick me up out the front and we can go on a picnic like we used to."

"Zinnia never came on a picnic with us."

"Well it's past time she did. And it's not like she hasn't done other things with us." She tried to remain calm, but it didn't look like their plan was going to work. She struggled not to panic.

"I'll pick you up out the front in a few minutes." Hazel sounded like she said the words by rote.

Aura clasped the handpiece with both hands.

"Tell her she doesn't sound like herself. Ask what is wrong." Riley spoke as softly as he'd done before.

She took a deep breath, trying desperately to remain calm. "What's wrong? You sound odd. Not like yourself."

Hazel laughed. A fake brittle sound like the woman had made earlier.

The sound sent a shiver through Aura and she swayed. Was her mum possessed?

Riley slipped an arm around her shoulders, meeting her gaze. "Threaten to leave." Again his words were whisper soft.

The compassion in his eyes steadied her. "That didn't answer either of my questions. Are you sure you're okay? Maybe we should go back to Brisbane. Pick me up and we'll head straight home."

"I will talk to Zinnia and see what she says. A picnic is a lot of work."

The words felt like a confirmation. Since when did her mum worry about work when it came to fun? "I'll make the picnic. All you have to do is pick me up and the three of us will eat it before going to Blue Sky. I wanted to share the spot with you like you've shared so many different locations with me. And with Aunt Zinnia since it's been so long since I've seen her. Normally you'd have jumped at the suggestions by now. Are you sure everything is okay?"

"I will talk to Zinnia and ring you back shortly."

Chapter Nine

Aura continued to hold the handpiece to her ear, shocked her mum had hung up so abruptly. She lowered it, not bothering to put it on the cradle. "How can you tell if someone is possessed? Other than they can't go onto hallowed ground."

Riley took the handpiece from her and hung it up, needing to take his arm from around her to do so. "What happened?"

"She hung up on me. Without saying goodbye or anything."

"That doesn't mean she's possessed. They could be ordering her about and telling her what to say and do. I have the feeling she'd be susceptible to demonic suggestions."

She momentarily closed her eyes, his words not making her feel any better.

"We will get them out of there. If this doesn't

work, we'll come up with another plan." Riley raised her left hand to waist height.

She opened her eyes to stare at his hand clasping hers, holding her hand so the mark on her wrist was visible. "I thought it was an insect bite. I didn't know I had it until I was walking down the hallway."

Riley chuckled. "You've banished demons. You will be able to rescue your family. Then you can take them home and away from this mess."

His suggestion sounded extremely tempting. "What about you?" She looked up from her wrist to meet his gaze. "You'll be left here alone to deal with the demons. Including one that has a personal vendetta against you."

Riley shrugged, his grin not dimming. "Comes with the territory. They tend to dislike being banished to hell."

"What about the one who threatened me? Do I have to worry about him?"

"Only if you continue to banish demons. If there are no demons who know who you are or where you live then he won't be able to track you down. And your demon mark isn't significant enough to catch the attention of demons."

The phone rang, making Aura jump. "Should I…"

It wasn't her phone and wouldn't necessarily be for her, but what if it was?

"Answer it," Riley said softly.

She waited until the next ring had finished before picking up the handpiece. "Hello?"

"Aura. Zinnia and I would love to have a picnic with you. We'll bring a bottle of wine to share and celebrate the three of us spending time together."

"Okay." She tried not to sound sceptical, but her mum didn't drink. She believed it messed with psychic powers. "I'll meet you out the front at midday."

"See you then." Hazel hung up.

"What did she say?" Riley took the handpiece from her again when she continued to clutch it.

"That can't have been my mum."

"Why not?"

"She doesn't drink and she's bringing a bottle of wine for us to share."

"Don't drink it. There could be anything in it. Including demon's blood."

"I–" she broke off, her legs starting to give way on her. She staggered to an armchair, shaking her head. "None of this should be possible." Avoiding looking at the photos scattered across the coffee table, her gaze was drawn to the demon mark on her wrist. "Impossible."

Riley squatted in front of her, taking her hands. "You're not alone."

Her gaze roamed over his face, seeing the seriousness and hearing the promise in his tone. It took her a moment to realise this was the most serious she'd seen him since they'd first met. "It's going to be bad, isn't it?"

"I have a feeling things won't be pretty."

"Are you going to warn me about what I'm in for or am I going in blind?"

"Your clothes are ready."

Aura turned in the armchair to see Judy stood in the doorway, a small pile of neatly folded clothes in her hands. "Thank you." She looked from Riley to Judy several times.

"There will be time for warnings later. Get changed and I'll start putting together food for the picnic," Riley said.

"There are freshly baked biscuits." Judy handed the clothes over to Aura, stepping out of the doorway.

"I'm not sure–"

Riley joined them. "Sounds good to me." He grinned. "Trust me. Once you taste Judy's biscuits you'll never hesitate again." He turned to Judy. "What flavour are they, love?"

"I made cinnamon as well as jam drops."

"Please tell me I don't have to wait until the picnic to have one." Riley took a step towards the kitchen. "Or two."

Judy laughed, swatting Riley on the arm. "Two better not mean half a dozen. You're as bad as my boys. "

Aura watched them walk down the hallway, chatting and laughing. How could Riley laugh when they were surrounded by danger? She didn't move until they were out of sight, hurrying to the bedroom to change into her clothes, relieved to get out of the too big t-shirt and boxers.

She left Riley's clothes on the bed, feeling guilty that someone had made the bed for her. More than likely it had been Judy. She doubted Colin would have done it. Grabbing her phone, she slipped it into a pocket even though there was no coverage in the area. A glance around the room showed the curtain had been drawn open and the light turned off. The room looked like no one had spent the night in it. Other than the clothes she'd left on the bed it was like she'd never been here. And they weren't hers. No one would miss her or her family. The rush of fear had her sitting heavily on the edge of the bed.

No one knew where they were and her mum randomly disappeared out of people's lives, coming and going, sometimes never returning. She clasped her hands together, trying desperately not to panic. That wouldn't save her family. What skills did she have that would help her face demons? She'd frozen, hadn't been able to continue reciting the prayer at one stage. What if there'd been a second demon? They would have attacked her before she could have done anything.

She tried to focus on what she was capable of doing. She could joust, feed two people on next to no money and had a good aim when it came to throwing daggers. Only one skill that would be of any use in the situation. Lowering her head, she covered her face with her hands. They were dead. Or doomed to be possessed. She had a feeling the first option might be the better one.

"What happened?"

Lowering her hands she stared at Riley, who stood in the doorway, a jam drop biscuit in his hand. "How many people die to demons each year?"

Riley joined her on the bed, facing her as he sat

next to her. "I'm not about to let anything happen to you."

"How can you say that? And why would you care?"

"It's my job." He held out the biscuit. "Hungry?" He grinned at her. "I nearly ate it. Better take it before I change my mind."

She stared at his overly handsome face. It had been what had made her wary. The murderer had been impossibly good looking, enough that he made Riley look ordinary. His eyes caught her attention. That was what the murderer had been missing. Emotions other than excitement reflected in his eyes. Riley might be grinning, but deep in his eyes she saw his compassion. "You care."

The grin faded. "Most people do."

"No, you care about what might happen to me. A stranger."

The grin reappeared. "We've banished demons together. I think that makes us more than strangers."

"You care." She didn't know why it should make her feel better, but it did. A smile formed and she rose to her feet. "And no matter how much you joke around, I know you care." She took a bite of the biscuit before slipping her feet into her sneakers and striding from the room. It was every bit as delicious as Riley had promised. Reaching the kitchen, she found it empty, turning at the sound of soft footsteps behind her. Finished her biscuit, she asked Riley, "Where is everyone?"

"Colin is muttering over the bike and Judy is bringing in the rest of the washing."

"Are they safe out there?"

Riley nodded. "There are no demons nearby. Judy will be inside in a few minutes and Colin will be able to see any demons coming. He's close enough to the house to retreat to it before they reach him." He gestured towards the hallway. "Ready to check out the picnic location?"

"Yeah." She also had questions she wanted to ask him, but she'd wait until there was no chance of anyone interrupting. Following him to the front door, she noticed a picnic basket on the verandah against the front wall of the house.

"It can stay there until later," Riley said when Aura paused by the basket.

She glanced at Colin as she got in the ute, grinning as he muttered and cursed, a smear of grease across his forehead. "Should you give him a hand?"

Riley started the ute, shaking his head, not answering until the noise of the ute had settled down a bit. "Apparently I get in the way." He glanced at her, grinning.

She chuckled. That sounded like something Colin would say. She waited until they were on the road and the drive less jarring before she spoke. "How do we use the holy water? Do we throw it on Mum and Aunt Zinnia?"

"We have them drink it."

"Uhmm, the holy water? Don't people dip their fingers in it?"

Riley chuckled. "This is basically blessed drinking water. Blessed salt added to it. None of the holy water hunters carry has been in a font. I'll put it in all the drinks in the picnic basket. And the coffee. Don't worry, we occasionally need to drink it so we make sure it's of drinking quality."

"Why do you need to drink it?"

"If a demon consumes your blood it breaks your tie with them. As painful for them as it is for the person breaking the tie."

"It'll hurt them?" She didn't want either of them hurt. Especially not her mum.

"It's better than the alternative."

She started to ask what the alternative was, but decided that wasn't necessary. She wanted to get both her mum and aunt away from the demons. "Is that all? They'll feel pain."

"And throw up blood."

"What?" She winced at her own shriek. "Blood?"

Riley pulled over, parking on the wide grassy shoulder of the road. He remained in the vehicle, facing Aura. "We don't know if the holy water will do anything to them. It's only if they have a tie to a demon. The hold Curtis has over them might only be in effect while he's with them or for short periods of time after. But the fact they're bringing a bottle of wine to share makes me think one, or both of them, has a strong tie to a demon. Or several demons."

"Blood." She couldn't get past the idea that a demon might have drunk their blood. "Demons drink blood. Like some sort of vampire?"

Riley chuckled. "Vampires don't exist. Blood gives demons power. Human blood that is."

She closed her eyes at the visions his words brought. It wasn't a good idea, the images becoming more vibrant in her mind. When his hand rested on her shoulder, she opened her eyes to see the compassion in his. "How much blood will they throw up?"

"That depends on how much of their blood demons have consumed."

Once more she found herself closing her eyes. Zinnia had been at Blue Sky for three months. A shudder ran through her.

"You're not alone, sweetheart." His words were soft.

She opened her eyes to see he grinned. A wry one formed on her lips. "You do that deliberately, don't you?"

He chuckled. "It works."

She didn't bother telling him it hadn't made her angry this time. Not now she knew what he was doing. Besides, he never used a patronising tone when he said the word. It had taken her a bit to realise. "What about when it no longer works?"

"I guess I'll have to start calling you love."

Her lips parted, but words didn't form. The way he'd said it had sounded far too good, especially with the soft tone of voice he'd used. Drawing in a shuddering breath, she glanced away. "We should check out the area before it's time to meet my family."

"It's the danger."

"What?" She looked at him over her shoulder, having started to open the door.

"What you're feeling. It's the danger."

"No. Not me. Danger and a pretty face tend to do the opposite. Life has taught me that." Life, murderers and pretty faces. She met his gaze. "You're different." As she'd already said, he cared. Not many people she met did. Or at least cared for others before themselves.

She opened the ute door, the creak breaking the silence.

Riley led the way to an overgrown graveyard, the fence half tumbling down, the headstones worn and cracked in places. "The stream is over there." He pointed beyond the headstones. "The hallowed ground is wide enough they'll have to go well out of their way to avoid it, making it obvious what they're doing."

"Where will you be?"

"That stand of trees over there." He pointed in the direction that Colin and Judy's place was in. "I can say I walked over with the thermos of coffee."

"Are you going to?"

He shrugged. "If I have to." A grin formed. "I'm hoping Colin will have the bike going again."

She chuckled. "You sure he'll let you use it after bringing it back broken?"

"Do you doubt my skills of persuasion?"

She was unable to answer him, her gaze drawn to his lips again. Why did he always have a ready smile and have to be so good looking? Although she doubted she'd feel any different even if he were the most ordinary person in the world. He intrigued her despite his looks.

"Is your silence your way of telling me how little you think of my abilities?"

"No." She glanced at the ute. "We should return. In case the ute breaks down and we find ourselves needing to walk."

Riley chuckled, leading the way to the ute. "It'll probably outlast the bike."

The drive to Colin and Judy's place was made in silence. There were so many questions she wanted answered, yet she was worried what answers he'd give. Maybe jumping into situations blind was the better option. How many times would she have thought twice about rescuing her mum if she'd known exactly how bad the situation was going to be? Who was she kidding? She might have thought twice about some of the situations, but she would have rescued her mum anyway.

Chapter Ten

They arrived back to find Colin had fixed the motorbike. Aura headed inside out of the heat, leaving Riley to convince Colin to let him borrow the motorbike again. She smiled at Colin's complaints, including the one that he needed to replace the headlights on the ute. Checking her phone, her steps slowed when she saw the time. Midday was rapidly approaching. She changed her mind about how quickly it was arriving when the minutes began to drag and it felt like hours instead of the hour it actually took before Riley gave her and the picnic basket a lift to the front gate. Getting off the bike, she returned the spare helmet to him and watched as he tied it on the back of the bike, giving her a nod and a grin before heading down the road towards the graveyard. She continued to look in that direction even after he was out of sight.

Ten minutes later her mum's car pulled up and she put the picnic basket on the back seat and leaned in the front window to smile at the two of them. "Hi, Mum. Aunt Zinnia. I'll drive. Easier than explaining where we're going." She opened the driver's door, stepping back to let Zinnia out.

"I'm sure I'm capable of following directions," Zinnia said curtly.

"But am I capable of giving them?" She forced a smile to her lips, trying not to think of all Riley had told her and everything she'd seen. "Surely you're not worried about my driving ability. I split the drive here with Mum."

"Get in the car, Aura." Zinnia's tone remained curt.

It took a lot of effort to keep her smile in place. Her aunt was never curt with her. More often than not it was the tone she used with Hazel. Meeting Zinnia's gaze, she was surprised at the plea she could see in her eyes. The dark brown eyes, several shades lighter than the colour of Zinnia's hair that was cut in a no nonsense style, darted away several times. Was Zinnia trying to tell her something?

"Aren't we going on a picnic?" Hazel leaned forward, her arm resting against her sister's.

"Please let me drive, Aunt Zinnia." Aura half expected her aunt to argue again.

Zinnia left the car running, unbuckling her seatbelt and getting in the back next to the picnic basket. "Ridiculous if you ask me. How hard is it to give directions?"

Relief rushed through her. She'd started to think the plan would fail before it had begun. "Thank you." She let her mum's babble wash over her, not caring about the many amazing people at Blue Sky. Hearing Feud's name mentioned a couple of times, as well as Havoc's, had her heart racing, but she remained silent. They'd be away from here soon enough. Thanks to Riley's help.

She pulled up on the wide shoulder near the graveyard and turned off the engine.

"We're here?" Hazel looked around. "I don't see a stream."

"It's not far." Aura got out of the car, waiting for Zinnia to get out of the back with the bottle of wine she held so she could collect the picnic basket.

"Open the boot, Aura. I need my hat." Hazel stood by the boot.

Aura left the picnic basket on the back seat and opened the boot, relieved to see all their gear remained scattered throughout it. This had to be one of the few times she was happy her mum was so disorganised. Remembering Riley's comment about hair dye and tattoos, her gaze was drawn to her mum's ankle. Relief rushed through her to see the butterfly looked the same as always, clearly visible above the straps of her mum's sandals. She leaned against the car as she tried to steady her breathing, not wanting Zinnia to notice anything was wrong. Her mum, as usual, was oblivious to most of what went on in front of her.

Once the boot was shut, the picnic basket collected off the back seat and the car locked, Aura led the way through the graveyard. She kept glancing at each of them, another burst of relief rushing through her when neither of them hesitated to enter the graveyard. Reaching the bank of the stream, she set the picnic basket down under the shade of a tree and opened it.

Hazel brushed her out of the way. "What a lovely picnic blanket." She took it out and spread it across the springy grass, smiling serenely. "We should do this more often."

"You're such a fool, Hazel." Zinnia glared at her sister as she dropped onto the blanket, starting to open the bottle of wine.

Before Aura could come up with a reason to stop Zinnia from opening the bottle, Riley came towards them, holding up the thermos.

"You forgot your coffee. Judy sent me with it."

Zinnia glared at Aura, the bottle remaining closed. "What happened to family only?"

Riley was close enough to hear. "I'm only the delivery boy." He grinned, turning to Aura. "Although I wouldn't mind a drink of the water packed in the basket earlier. The day is scorching."

"That sounds like a good idea." Aura took the thermos and sat it beside the basket, rummaging around in it for cups and the bottle of water. She needed to take out several items before she could reach the bottle.

"Now you mention it, I could do with a drink of water. I might even paddle in the stream once we've eaten." Hazel took the plastic cup Aura filled.

Aura filled another one and held it out to Zinnia. "We should have the wine with the food. Don't you always say it's foolish to drink on an empty stomach?"

Zinnia took the cup, an expression of annoyance on her face. "Since when have you bothered listening to me?" She took a mouthful of the water. The cup fell from her hand, spilling across the blanket as she clutched at her stomach, her eyes widening. "What did you do?"

Riley grabbed an empty container out of the picnic basket, holding it out to Zinnia. "Sorry."

Zinnia started to speak, grabbing the container instead and throwing up into it.

"Zinnia?"

Aura grabbed her mum's hand when she started to reach for Zinnia. "Don't." Fear arrowed through her at the amount of blood Zinnia threw up. Easily two cups. Was that bad? She didn't know and wasn't sure if she should ask.

"They'll know." Zinnia looked directly at Riley. "I have to go before they come after me."

"No." Aura shook her head. "You can't go back to them. You have to come home with us. Home to Brisbane."

"They have my blood. I'm not going anywhere."

Aura stared at her aunt, the words echoing in her head, the images of the slaughtered livestock again replaced with images of her aunt. "No." She moved closer to Zinnia. "You can't go back there."

Zinnia rested her hand on Aura's cheek, smiling sadly. "I wouldn't want you caught up in this mess." She looked past Aura. "You take your daughter and get out of here. There's no way I want either of you caught up with demons."

"Demons?" Hazel asked.

Aura nearly groaned at her mum's tone. The earlier fear was replaced with curiosity.

"How clueless are you? What did you think was going on there? Demons, Hazel. Creatures from hell."

Hazel smiled serenely. "I always knew such things existed. I wonder what they could tell us about hell. Do people really get sent there when they die?"

"For once in your life do the sensible thing." Zinnia's tone was sharp, her gaze remaining on her sister. "Return to Brisbane and take Aura with you. Think of her for a change."

"Aren't you going with us?" Hazel asked.

"Haven't you been listening?" Zinnia demanded. "They have my blood. No matter where I go, they'll track me down. Do you think I'd lead demons to Aura?" She stumbled to her feet. "I have to go before they come after me." She grabbed Aura's hands. "Take your useless mother and get away from here as fast as you can. Promise me that."

There'd been more than a handful of times throughout her life when she'd wished Zinnia was her mother. Sensible, organised and always there when you needed her. She wasn't about to desert her. "I won't fail you."

"Good. Take care of her." Zinnia glanced at Hazel. "Someone has to. Sorry it has to be you."

Aura watched Zinnia stride away, her hand pressed

to her stomach. She ignored her mum's complaints about how her sister had spoken to and about her.

Riley came to stand beside Aura. "They won't be left there. None of them. Not even your aunt."

She met his gaze, seeing the compassion in his warm, brown eyes. "She's in pain."

Riley inclined his head. "She's a strong woman."

Aura nodded. "She always has been."

Hazel's complaints ended abruptly. "Do demons grant wishes?"

Aura was tempted to yell at her mum. Her hands curled into fists and she opened her mouth, even though she doubted anything she could say would distract her mum from discovering the answer to her question. The hard way.

Riley smiled, holding out a hand to Hazel and drawing her a few steps away from the picnic blanket. "You don't want to go doing anything silly like messing with demons."

"Do they grant wishes though?"

"They're not a genie," Aura muttered.

Riley's smile vanished. "The only wish demons will guarantee to grant you is death. And not an easy one either."

Hazel took half a step away, her smile faltering.

"They couldn't have been demons. Everyone at Blue Sky is human."

"Feud is a demon." Aura moved closer to her mum, fighting the urge to grab hold of her shoulders and shake her. Hard. "He wants to kill Riley."

Hazel slowly shook her head. "Impossible. He was such a gentleman. He'd never hurt anyone."

Aura gritted her teeth together on all the names she could have spoken. Starting with that of a murderer, a serial killer in the making. Her anger faded as she realised a way to save Zinnia. She turned to Riley. "Your blood–"

Riley interrupted. "You and your mum should leave."

"I'm not about to leave my sister here."

"I'll stay, Mum. You can't help. You'd only end up in more trouble."

"I came here to see my sister. I'm not going until I finish spending time with her." Hazel began to make a circling motion with her hands.

Aura grabbed hold of her mum's hands. "The universe will not save you from demons."

Hazel met Aura's glare. "How do you know?"

"Unless you renamed me 'Universe' without telling me, it hasn't helped you once since you started this stupid 'bubble it'. I have dealt with every single problem."

Hazel tugged her hands from Aura's grip, a hurt expression on her face. "That's cruel, Aura."

"So is relying on the universe to solve your problems. Go back to Brisbane and try and stay out of trouble while I rescue Aunt Zinnia."

"She was my sister long before she was your aunt."

Riley stepped closer so he was almost between them. "Can you take a message to my family in Brisbane? There are things they need to know, but I'm worried the phone lines might be tapped. There's no one else I can trust to take a message to them."

"Tapped?" Excitement filled Hazel's eyes. "Like on a crime show?"

Riley grinned. "Exactly. So what do you say? Can you help me out?"

"I really should stay." Hazel's words were hesitant.

Riley took both of Hazel's hands, meeting her gaze. "It'd mean a great deal if you could help me, sweetheart."

Aura nearly rolled her eyes at the smile her mum gave Riley.

"This will help?"

"You have no idea exactly how much it will help me."

About all it would help with was getting her mum out of the way. Aura managed to keep the words to herself. But it was an effort.

"I suppose I could drive back to Brisbane and give them your message. It's not that long a drive. I can stay the night at home and come back tomorrow."

Before Aura could protest that plan, Riley spoke.

"That would be perfect. I don't suppose you have a pen and paper in your car."

Aura followed them to the car. How hard was it to deal with a handful of demons and a cult? Could this be sorted before her mum got back tomorrow? She watched as Riley scribbled on the scrap of paper her mum found in the car. "What does Hebrews 2:18 mean?" Beneath it he'd written an address in Brisbane.

Riley handed the scrap of paper and pen to Hazel. "It's a verse from the Bible. My family will know what I mean."

"Ooh. It's a code. How exciting." Hazel stared at the scrap of paper.

Riley held the driver's door open. "Go straight to their place. Don't stop here for anything. Actually, only stop for fuel between here and Brisbane. Not for any other reason. We don't want the demons stopping you from getting that message to my family."

Aura took her smaller bag from the boot before handing the car keys over to her mum, hugging her tightly. "Be careful."

Hazel smiled serenely. "I'm sure the universe will take care of everything. With very little help from us."

Chapter Eleven

Aura tried to smile, but it felt more like a grimace. She managed not to speak the words that her mum wouldn't listen to and waved as Hazel started the car. She stood beside Riley, waiting until her mum was out of sight before she spoke. "What was the message you sent?"

"For the suffering he himself passed through while being put to the test enables him to help others when they are being put to the test."

She faced him, confused by his reply. "That doesn't tell me what the message is."

"It's a quote from the Bible."

"I get that part. But what does it mean to your family?"

Riley grinned. "That hopefully they'll be able to keep her out of trouble and from coming back here while there are demons in the area."

"If they can do that, they're miracle workers."

Riley chuckled. "Gran's pretty canny. She's outsmarted a lot of demons over the years. I'm sure she can handle your mum." He gestured in the direction of where they'd left their picnic. "You hungry?"

"Not really. We should pack it up." She strode back to the picnic blanket, stopping abruptly when she spotted the container Zinnia had thrown up in. "Can we get rid of that?"

Riley put a lid on the container, shaking his head. "The blood needs to be dealt with properly so no demon can get hold of it." He sat on the blanket and helped himself to the food.

She stared open mouthed at him, finally managing to speak. "You're not going to eat, are you?"

"I'm not about to go hungry." Riley grinned before he took another bite of food.

"But…" She gestured towards the closed container.

"If I let a little blood stop me eating I'd frequently be hungry."

Little? Two cups weren't exactly little. But she didn't bother saying that. She didn't think she wanted to learn what a demon hunter considered a lot of blood. Remaining standing felt awkward so she sat beside him, leaving her small bag at the edge of the blanket and avoiding the wet patch where Zinnia had spilled the water. "What about the bottle of wine? What are we going to do with it?"

Riley grinned. "Certainly not drink it."

"Be serious."

"Me? I wouldn't have a clue how to be serious. Which is why one of the hunters gave me the nickname Jester."

She examined his face, finding the seriousness she was wanting deep in his eyes. "Don't they know you very well?"

Riley chuckled, holding out a jam drop. "Oh, he knows me very well." He paused. "Can I tempt you with a biscuit?"

She nearly blurted out that he could tempt her with a lot of things. Taking the biscuit, she took a bite rather than let the words escape. Her gaze was drawn to the closed container and she tried not to think about what was in it. Forcing herself to look away, her attention was caught by the scenery. The last thing she'd expected when she joined her mother on this trip was to be sitting on a picnic blanket with a good-looking guy in a romantic setting. Or at least it was romantic looking if she didn't glance behind her at the graveyard or think about what was in the container. She automatically took the sandwich Riley handed her when she finished the biscuit. "How do you do this?"

"Do what?"

She made a gesture that vaguely encompassed the area. "Relax knowing that all this is an illusion. The beauty of this area hides…" Her voice trailed off. There was no way she could put into words what she'd seen in those photos.

"The beauty of this area is a completely separate thing from what is happening here. It's a location, nothing more. You can find demons anywhere. In war-torn countries, in a poverty stricken area, in an ancient castle or here, amongst these rolling hills and perfect views."

His words played over in her mind as she absently ate the sandwich. Finishing the last bite, she faced him again. "What are you going to do with the bottle of wine?"

"Cleanse it. Along with the blood." Riley rose to his feet. "I'll bring the bike closer while you start packing up."

"What if I want to get the motorbike and leave you to pack up?"

"Do you know where I left it?"

She glared up at him.

Grinning, Riley strode away.

She returned everything to the basket, leaving out only the bottle of wine and container of blood. They made her think of Riley's blood and how it was the only way to lead Feud away from the area. When Riley returned with the motorbike, she took the helmet he held out to her and put it on. "Why did you stop me earlier when I started to talk about your blood?"

"I wasn't certain I could convince Hazel to return to Brisbane. She doesn't strike me as the sort of person who knows when to keep a secret."

She wanted to defend her mum, but his analysis was too accurate. "Do you still want to lead Feud away?"

Riley picked up the picnic basket, slipping the bottle of wine inside. "We'll go back to Colin and Judy's before we discuss it. There are demons headed this way." He swung his leg over the seat of the motorbike, sitting the basket in front of him. "Can you grab the container?"

She stared at the container of blood. It was the last thing she wanted to do.

"You might want to hurry. Most of my weapons are in my room."

She gingerly picked up the container and her bag and got on behind him. "Most?"

Riley chuckled. "Hunters never go anywhere completely unarmed."

"What would you have said yesterday if I took you up on your offer to search you for weapons?"

"You wouldn't have." He started the motorbike. "Hold on."

She'd barely wrapped one arm around him, her arm through the handles of the bag, her grip tightening on the container, before he took off. She held tighter, pretty certain he was going over the speed limit. They were back at the old house within minutes, a trail of dust following them down the driveway. As soon as the engine was turned off, Aura got off the motorbike.

"Inside." Riley missed every second step, taking the helmet off as he went. He looked over his shoulder. "Hurry."

After scanning the area, and seeing nothing, she followed him inside. "What is happening?"

Riley sat the picnic basket and his helmet down in the hallway. "If it was night, I'd say a powerful demon was coming. Since it's day, there must be quite a few minor ones."

Judy stepped out of her bedroom, her smile disappearing when she looked them over. "Did something happen?"

"Is Colin inside? Demons are coming."

"I'll check and see if he's in the kitchen." Judy hurried down the hallway.

Aura left her gear and the blood beside the picnic basket, following Riley into the lounge room. "What are we going to do?"

He didn't answer her, using the rotary dial once he'd lifted up the handset of the phone. "Hi, Gran. I've sent a, shall we call it a package, your way?"

Aura strained to hear the other end of the conversation, but could only hear a murmur.

"Keep it for me. Distraction should work." Riley chuckled, pausing a moment before he spoke again. "You'll recognise the quote." Again he chuckled. "Okay, Gran. You too." Riley hung up the phone.

Before Aura could once again ask him what they were going to do, Judy burst into the lounge room.

"He's gone to fix that fence at the back of the next paddock."

"Don't worry about it, love." Riley briefly wrapped an arm around Judy's shoulders. "I'll see him safely back to the house." He strode from the room.

Aura hurried after him. "You said there are a lot coming."

Riley nodded gathering his sword, bow and quiver. "I'm not about to leave him out there alone." He grabbed a handful of vials filled with holy water and put them in his pockets.

"You can't go out there on your own." She grabbed hold of his arm when he tried to leave the room.

"It's okay, sweetheart. You'll be safe if you stay inside." He tugged his arm from her grip and started for the door.

"It no longer works, sweetheart."

He glanced over his shoulder with a grin. "You sure, love?"

She slowly shook her head as he walked away. She must be crazy. Grabbing the throwing daggers and vials of holy water she ran after him. Once the vials were tucked in pockets, she held a dagger in each hand. She didn't slow her pace until she'd caught up with Riley. Not that she was able to slow her pace by much. Riley's long legged stride carried him across the yard. She glanced at him. "I'm sure. Love."

Riley chuckled. "It's a habit. When you rescue people from demons they usually need a little comfort. And they don't always tell you their name."

"You know my name."

"I know. But sometimes–" He broke off at the sound of a gunshot, breaking into a run.

Aura tried to keep up with him, but he was faster

than her. She came over a rise and spotted Colin by a fence, a gate open, his rifle raised as a demon strode towards him. She had no doubt it was a demon with its leathery wings spread behind it and equally leathery skin.

The demon rushed towards Colin, knocking him from his feet, clawed hand raised to attack.

Riley drew an arrow, firing at the demon as he continued to run towards it. "Go back to where you came from."

The demon hissed, staggering back from Colin to face Riley. "You will be outnumbered in minutes."

"Colin, get back to the house." Riley drew back another arrow.

Colin stumbled to his feet, shooting the demon when he came towards him again. His shot was followed by an arrow from Riley.

Aura slowly shook her head as she realised once again she stood frozen. She was going to end up getting herself killed at this rate. Remembering their earlier fights, she started to pray aloud, backing up when Riley did so, Colin now beside them. A glance around the area showed more demons approaching. She counted six. Then five more came up over a rise and she stumbled on the words of the prayer. They were dead. There was no way they could survive so many demons. Yet she kept praying, retreating with the other two who continued to fire at the demon, not knowing what else she could do.

When the demon Riley attacked vanished in a rush of flames, he faced the oncoming demons, another arrow ready. "Keep praying and stay together." He shot one of the oncoming demons who barely paused to rip the arrow from his body before continuing to come towards them. Riley glanced at Aura. "You watch our backs. And Colin you keep an eye out to the side." He faced the direction of the house.

She wanted to argue the need to walk backwards when they were so far from safety, but she doubted she'd be able to take her gaze from the approaching demons anyway. She continued to pray. The question she did want to ask, like how they would manage to survive, would involve no longer praying. She wasn't about to stop. Not when it was one of the few things she was capable of doing to help them survive the oncoming demons.

"We're not going to make it." Colin fired at a demon. He drew the bolt back, the spent cartridge was ejected before he slipped another five cartridges in, that he'd taken from his pocket. "The house is too far away."

"The situation isn't impossible yet."

She glanced at Riley. Was he serious? There were eleven demons striding towards them. All various shapes and sizes.

"When I give the word, you two run to the house." Riley slid an arm through the bow and slipped it over his head so it sat crosswise over his chest and back.

She couldn't hold back her questions any longer. "What about you? You don't expect us to leave you behind, do you?"

"Run." Riley spun, drawing his sword and attacking the demons.

Aura automatically ran with Colin, slowing as she realised Riley wasn't following. Turning, she saw he was surrounded, his rapidly swinging sword all that kept the demons from reaching him, his voice ringing out clearly in prayer.

"You're going to get yourself killed," Colin warned.

"We can't leave him there."

"It's his job. He was the one that came to us and said he could help." Colin shrugged. "We'll only get in the way."

Chapter Twelve

As Aura watched, Riley stumbled, one of the demons nearly getting him. Yet his voice didn't falter. "I can't let him die." Not to save her. She'd never forgive herself if she walked away and left him to die. Moving towards Riley, she began to pray, her voice echoing his. She threw one of the daggers, hitting a demon in the back between bony shoulder blades. He spun to face her. Grabbing out a vial of holy water, she tossed that at him as he came closer, not faltering in her praying. Beside her Colin fired his rifle, the empty cartridge ejected onto the ground as he drew the bolt back.

The demon continued to come for her. She threw the second dagger. It struck him in the chest. He ripped the dagger free and started to throw it at her. For a split second she froze, expecting the dagger to strike her.

Before the demon could throw the dagger, Colin fired again and the demon jerked backwards.

Not knowing what else to do Aura launched herself at the demon, knocking him to the ground and wrenching the dagger from his hand. She plunged it into him, continuing to pray, all the time expecting the long claws to sink into her flesh. She collapsed on the ground as the demon vanished like he'd never been there, startled enough that words failed her and she couldn't think what came next in the prayer. She was alive. Struggling to get up, she saw two demons coming towards them. The number of demons Riley fought had lessened. And not only by the one she'd banished and the two that came for them. She grabbed the dagger off the ground, still holding onto the one she'd plunged into the demon, her heart racing as she stood her ground.

"Sure you don't want to run?" Colin stepped up beside her, putting another five cartridges in his rifle.

Before she could reply, Riley knocked back one of the demons attacking him, forcing him into the other three left nearby. He spun and ran towards them, stopping his praying long enough to shout, "Go."

With a glance at the demons gaining on them, she ran towards the house, keeping pace with Colin. Riley reached them before the demons, continuing to pray. She joined him in the words, not daring to stop even though they were broken from running. The house was coming closer, Judy visible at the back door, the screen door open. Behind she heard the sound of the demons following.

Riley spun to face the oncoming demons. "Keep going. Don't stop this time." He returned to praying.

She hesitated, sharing a look with Colin, who shrugged. Putting some more distance between her and the demons first, she pointed to a demon with his back to them. "Shoot him." He was too far away for her dagger to do much damage. But as soon as he was closer, then she'd show him what she was capable of. Images of the one she'd attacked earlier filled her mind, a smile slowly forming. They might actually survive. She returned to praying aloud.

Colin fired at the demon several times before he was close enough for Aura to attack. She followed the dagger up with her last vial of holy water before the demon was nearly upon them. Colin swung the rifle at the demon, the timber butt hitting him.

While the demon was distracted with Colin, she attacked with the second dagger, throwing it at his eye, not sure if she should back up or grab the dagger on the ground at the demon's feet.

The demon roared, clawing at his face.

"That works a treat." Colin backed up as he took aim. Shooting the demon in the other eye.

Aura looked between the demon and the dagger, poised to run should he make a move in her direction.

Riley ran towards them, swinging his sword at the injured demon. The demon spun to face him, shattering into dust when Riley struck him again. "Don't you pair listen?"

Aura barely glanced at the demons who were regrouping and coming after them. If she focused on them for too long she was likely to run. There were too many of them and her heart pounded loudly, reminding her that somehow she lived. "I'm not about to listen when you give stupid orders." She collected her daggers before running with Riley and Colin towards the house. A glance over her shoulder showed the remaining four demons were gaining on them. They weren't going to make it. The house wasn't close enough. In the doorway Judy continued to watch them, her hands gripping the doorframe. She wanted to tell Colin to keep running, to go back to his wife, but she didn't want to stop praying again. Not with how close the demons were. She didn't know if it was helping, but since Riley continued to pray, she guessed that somehow it must.

Riley stopped and faced the demons, pausing in his praying long enough to say, "Keep going."

Aura grinned, even though there was nothing at all to laugh about. Did he honestly think they'd leave him behind? She waited until there was some distance between them and the demons before she pointed out one for Colin to shoot. The demon roared, but continued to attack Riley. She pointed at him again. Once more the demon roared, but remained focused on his current prey.

Colin shot the demon four more times, needing to reload during his attack, before the demon vanished. Colin shared a look with Aura, shrugging.

She shrugged too, not sure what had happened. Why hadn't the demon come after them? Not that it mattered. There were three left and Riley appeared to be slowing down. She pointed out another demon. This one did come after them. They backed away, Colin firing at it and Aura throwing the daggers once it was close enough. The words of the prayer became difficult to remember when the demon ripped the daggers from his body, tossing them aside, well out of reach. She was unarmed and an angry demon stalked towards her, barely bothered by Colin's shots.

Colin fired again. The demon jerked slightly. "Better make a run for it. I'll cover your retreat."

She wasn't about to desert them. Looking around for something to use as a weapon, she spied a fallen branch. It was three metres long and jagged on one end, most of the smaller branches having been broken in the fall from the nearby gum tree. It looked like her jousting ability might not be a waste after all. Again the words of the prayer failed her as she struggled not to give into panic. She grabbed the makeshift lance and ran at the demon with it. The smell of smouldering fires washed over her.

The demon roared when the jagged end impaled him, trying to wrench it from his body.

She kept pressure on it, terrified of what he might do if he came close. The murderous look in his flame filled eyes gave her a good idea of what that might be. Her arms ached and she braced her legs, pushing the branch as hard as possible into the demon.

The demon roared again, hands outstretched. Unable to reach her, dark blood pouring down his chest, the demon brought his hands together above the branch. A sword formed.

Aura's mouth opened, no sounds formed. She was dead. The sound of the rifle had the demon jerking, but it didn't stop him from drawing back the sword. Aura pressed the branch harder against the demon, her arms trembling from the effort.

Colin shot the demon again, Riley running towards them, shouting at them to go.

Aura couldn't stop. Couldn't let go. The words of the prayer came back to her and she recited them aloud as the sword swung towards her. The world seemed to slow. Sunlight glinted on the blade as she heard the rifle again.

The demon burst into flames, gone within seconds, the end of her lance on fire. She stared at where he'd been, stunned she was still alive.

"Run," Riley ordered.

Holding onto the branch, she turned and ran towards the house, not about to leave a burning branch behind when it might start a bushfire.

Colin pointed to a trough of water near the gate leading into the smaller house yard. "Drop the end in there."

Reaching the trough, she did as Colin had ordered, her arms continuing to ache. The branch was thicker than a typical lance and a fair bit heavier. A glance behind showed there were two demons left. She wanted to yell at them to leave. She couldn't fight anymore. She was exhausted.

Riley grabbed hold of her arm and dragged her into the house yard. "Keep moving. Get inside." His breathing was heavy.

Another glance showed the demons were gaining on them. She ran, forcing her protesting body to obey. Colin reached the house first and she staggered inside after him, drawing Riley in when he stumbled up the stairs. The two of them collapsed on the floor, Riley's sword beside them.

"They didn't get you?" Riley half rose, his gaze scanning her body. "No blood left behind?"

"No." All her aches were from throwing herself at demons and landing on the ground when they vanished. She was surprised that somehow she'd avoided getting demon blood on herself. Sitting up, she brushed dirt and leaves from her clothes, looking past Riley to see the two demons in the yard. "What are we going to do about them?"

"Shoot them once I catch my breath." Colin sat at the table, cradling his rifle, leaning forward to rest his arms on his knees. "I might be old, but there's plenty of fight left in me."

"You old fool." Judy put a glass of water and a box of cartridges on the table beside Colin, fondness in her tone.

"Who you calling an old fool?" Colin grumbled as he grabbed the glass, having a drink before reloading and putting more cartridges in the pockets of his trousers.

Riley took the glass Judy held out to him, grinning. "Don't suppose you've got more of them biscuits."

"You're hungry? We've not long eaten." Aura took the glass of water Judy held out to her. Her hands trembled from exhaustion so she wrapped both of them around it.

Riley's grin was replaced by seriousness. "Are you sure you're okay?"

She nodded then took a mouthful of water as she tried to organise her thoughts. "Is it always like this?"

Riley grinned. "That was nothing. I've faced worse than that before."

She shuddered. "How are you still alive?"

Again he sobered. "Not all hunters manage to live a long life."

She wanted to say something reassuring, but nothing seemed right. If he continued to face demons alone, then he was likely to have a short life too. "Why don't you have help?"

He glanced through the screen door. "As if I need help to face this lot." He placed the glass on the floor before staggering to his feet. "Did you hear that, demons? Go tell your master I will take him down. Alone. I can take anything you try and throw at me."

"Pride, hunter?" One of the demons came closer. "Do your lot not consider that a sin?"

"Pride? Not at all. Fact. Both you and my cousin are wrong."

The second demon chuckled. "Now we understand. The pride of youth. Does your book not say it comes before a fall?"

"It's not pride when you're confident of your own skill." He pointed at the demon through the screen. "Tell your master I'm coming for him."

The demons shared a look, the second one chuckling again. "You can't even leave the house. Do not worry. I will take your message to him. He enjoys a good laugh." The second demon strode away, leaving his companion behind.

"You might want to leave too," Riley said. "It'll save you the pain of being banished to hell."

The demon laughed. "You can barely hold yourself upright. Look how you cling to that wall."

Aura placed her glass next to Riley's and staggered to her feet, angered by the demon's taunts. "There are two of us against the one of you."

Colin walked heavily over to join them. "Three." He clutched his rifle, glaring at the demon.

"That is it?" The demon sneered. "Three humans, only one of you a hunter."

Judy joined them, a spray bottle in her hands. "Think I'll stand back and watch you destroy my home?" She squeezed the trigger of the spray bottle and the long stream reached the demon.

He stumbled backwards, snarling. "You will regret that."

Judy sprayed him again. "I doubt it."

Aura grinned when the demon stumbled further back. "I want a spray bottle of holy water too. No, actually I want a water blaster. One of those really powerful ones."

"There are a couple in the laundry from when my boys had their little ones out here last year," Judy said.

Aura felt a burst of energy at the thought of getting the water blasters, a smile curving her lips. She wasn't about to let a demon have her cowering in the house. She turned to Riley. "What do you say?"

He chuckled. "Let me get my sword."

"I need more holy water." She thought of the daggers she'd left behind. The water blaster would do for now.

Judy crossed the room and took a bottle of water from the cupboard, holding it out to Aura. "I have two more left." A cross had been drawn on the bottle with a black marker pen.

"Thanks." She looked from Riley to the demon who kept out of range. "Ready to do this?"

Riley grinned. "I'm always ready to banish

demons." He pushed the screen door open, his sword in hand as he strode down the stairs.

"In the cupboard straight across from the door," Judy said. "Top shelf."

"I'm right behind you." Colin fired at the demon, who snarled, running towards them.

"Go, Aura." Riley raised his sword, praying aloud as he met the demon halfway.

She ran, not wanting to leave them facing the demon without her help. By the time she found the water blasters and filled one with the bottle of holy water, the demon was gone and she stared at where he'd been. "I wanted to use the water blaster on him."

Riley laughed. "I'm sure you'll have more than enough chances before we get your aunt back." He nodded towards the house. "Come inside and we'll figure out how to go about that while there are no demons around to hear our plans."

She scanned the area. "Are you sure they're gone?"

He gestured towards her wrist. "Even you might be able to notice some of them now."

Her gaze was drawn to her wrist, surprised to see the demon mark had lengthened slightly. "I didn't notice."

"It would have been while we fought in the paddock."

His words reminded her of the daggers. "I need to collect my daggers. They're still out there." Her body ached and she wanted to collapse. Straightening her shoulders, she refused to give into the urge.

"I'll get the daggers. You two start planning. The sooner we get rid of these creatures the sooner we can bring our livestock home." Colin strode towards the open gate at the back of the yard.

Chapter Thirteen

Aura joined Riley at the table, Judy bustling around the kitchen as she started dinner. The spray bottle of holy water was on the kitchen bench by the sink. Aura put the water blaster in front of her on the table. "Did you mean what you said about your cousin being wrong? Are you here alone?"

"We don't want them believing help is on the way." Riley grinned. "And I never actually said what my cousin is wrong about. It isn't necessarily the same thing the demon is wrong about."

"Do you want to lead Feud away?"

"Yeah, but I'm not sure what to do with him after that. I'll probably have to call in help to take care of things here while I keep him away."

Judy glanced over her shoulder. "I didn't mind that Emily. Dan was okay too."

Riley shrugged. "It'll depend on what else is

happening. They might be busy doing other things. I have other family members you'll like as much as them."

"We'll see." Judy returned her attention to the vegetables she was peeling.

"So I can offer your blood to Feud in exchange for Aunt Zinnia?" Aura asked.

"You have to make certain you ask for both her and anything that belongs to her. We can't leave her blood with them or they'll be able to find her. Once we have her away from there we'll break any further ties they've created between her and the demons."

She met his gaze, pretty certain she knew what he meant, but wanting to know for certain. "You're going to make her drink holy water again."

"Yeah."

"What's to stop them from hurting either of you during the exchange?" Judy asked.

"I can't go or none of this will work." Riley continued to meet Aura's gaze. "You would be doing this on your own. Can you manage that?"

She swallowed hard, nodding when her voice failed her. She wasn't about to leave her aunt with demons.

"Tell them I was injured in the fight and you kept the cloth you used to tend my wound. You'll have to ring after dark. Feud won't be there yet. He's too strong to be about in the daylight." Riley reached across the table and took her hand, squeezing it lightly. "Which means you're going to have to travel to the graveyard on your own when it's night."

"Can't I make the exchange here?" Aura asked.

"You can't send her out there on her own," Judy protested.

Colin came in the back door, holding the two daggers in one hand, his rifle in the other. "What lame idea have you come up with this time?"

"He wants that poor girl to go out in the dark when there are demons wandering around," Judy said.

"There are demons wandering around in the day." Aura wasn't sure what the difference was, other than she wouldn't be able to see them coming.

"Weak demons," Judy said. "The ones who come out at night are more powerful."

"Oh." She had no idea what to say. Or do. If the ones she'd faced earlier were weak, she had no chance of surviving powerful demons.

"We can come up with another plan," Riley said.

She met his warm, brown eyes, seeing the compassion in them. "What if you weren't here? What if you were stuck somewhere safe, after dark, and couldn't get back?"

Riley grinned. "That bike."

Aura ignored Colin's mutters that there was nothing wrong with the motorbike. "Yes. Is there somewhere safe you could wait that they couldn't hurt you?"

"The graveyard."

"I'll pack you enough food to see you through the night," Judy said.

"I'll get the swag out of the shed." Colin put the daggers on the table. "I cleaned them for you. The same way the boy taught me." He started for the door.

Riley rose from his seat, shaking his head. "It can't seem planned." He turned to Judy. "Not too much food. Enough I won't go hungry, but not so much it'll look like I'd planned to stay out for the night. Probably a couple of tools so I can tinker around with the bike to make it look realistic. And a torch."

It didn't take Riley long to prepare for the evening and destroy the blood and wine they'd brought back with them. He sat at the table having an early meal that Judy made for him, his weapons resting across the end of the table. "Make sure you organise the meeting for an hour before daybreak. I need to be able to get back here and start planning my next move."

"What is our next move?" Aura asked.

"My next move." Riley stressed the first word. "I'll call my brother and let him know what's happening."

"The lines aren't tapped?"

Riley grinned. "It got your mum to leave, didn't it? And it's always possible they are."

"You lied to my mum."

"I'll do penance later. Once everyone is safe and Curtis has been dealt with."

Judy placed a lunchbox and thermos on the table. "The day is getting on. You should ring your family."

"It's about two hours till dark." Colin sat at the table, a cup of coffee and a couple of biscuits in front of him. "Don't go breaking the bike with those tools I put in the saddlebag for you."

Riley grinned. "Might even be able to improve it."

Aura laughed at Colin's expression and warnings. Her laughter faded at the thought of the coming night. "Will you be okay out there?"

"It won't be the first time I've spent the night in a graveyard." Riley grinned. "As long as it doesn't rain I'll be okay."

"What happens if it rains?" She half expected him to say the rain would interfere with the graveyard's ability to keep demons out.

"I'll get wet." Riley chuckled when Aura glared at him.

Judy cleared away Riley's empty plate. "Go ring your family and stop teasing the poor girl."

Riley left his bow and quiver on the table, taking only his sword. He caught hold of Aura's hand and drew her out of the kitchen with him. "You sure you're up to this? I can figure out another way to lead Feud away."

"What about Aunt Zinnia?"

"I'll find a way to save her too. To save all of them." He left his sword against the wall near the lounge room doorway.

She stared into his eyes, seeing the compassion and promise in them. "No. I'll help." She wasn't about to leave him to face them on his own. An image of him surrounded by demons, his sword swinging rapidly, came to mind. Not that he wasn't capable. He obviously was. "I can do this." The image of Riley with his rapidly swinging sword was replaced by one of her impaling the demon with her makeshift lance. A smile formed. "I can do this." She stressed the second word.

Riley nodded, picking up the handpiece of the vintage phone and using the rotary dial. "Hey, Blake." Riley chuckled. "What makes you think I've done something stupid?" He chuckled again, pausing before he answered. "Or about to do something stupid."

Aura stared at Riley. He was about to do something stupid? At least it sounded like his family thought he was. She started to speak, wanting to tell him they'd come up with a new plan.

"I need you here, Blake. Nothing can be done about Curtis while he has Feud's help." Riley paused, nodding. "Okay." He outlined what had been going on, not once mentioning the plan.

Aura frowned at a few quotes that sounded like they came from the Bible and she nearly asked him what they meant, deciding to wait until he was off the phone.

"Okay. I'll see you in the morning. If you can do something about my lack of transport too, that'd be great. It's frustrating only having the use of a motorbike that breaks down all the time." Riley chuckled again. "Mum and Gran will get over it." Another pause. "Okay, you too."

Aura spoke the moment he hung up the phone. "Are you planning to do something stupid?"

Riley grinned. "What makes you ask that?"

"I heard you. Now tell me. Are you going to do something stupid?"

"My family worry more than they need to, sweetheart."

"Really? Sweetheart."

Riley's grin vanished and he stepped close, taking one of her hands. "Do not step outside the house. No matter what happens. Understand?"

Fear flashed through her at his serious expression and equally serious tone. "I'm not stupid."

"Demons can mess with your head. You won't necessarily be seeing what you think you are."

"Okay."

"As long as you remain inside you're safe from demons."

"But not from humans."

Riley didn't answer immediately. "No."

"Better get going." Colin remained in the doorway for only a few seconds before his heavy footsteps could be heard heading towards the kitchen.

"Be careful." Riley released her hand and removed a bloodstained cloth from his pocket, placing it in her hand before he took a step away.

She started to tell him to be careful too, changing her mind to follow him and catch hold of his hand, slipping the cloth into her pocket. Moving close, she stared up at him for a moment before she leaned in and lightly brushed her lips across his.

He remained close to her, his voice soft. "It's the danger."

"No." She spoke as softly. "I've been in plenty of danger before." She let go of his hand to slide her hands around his neck, sinking against him. As her lips met his again, she felt his hands splay across her back, holding her close. Eventually she drew away, smiling as she met his gaze. "Be careful."

His expression remained serious as his gaze travelled across every inch of her face, eventually returning to her eyes. "Don't leave the house until I return. That won't be until the sun rises. And whatever you do, don't make any other deals with the demons." He held her a moment longer. Letting go, he took a step back, his gaze continuing to meet hers, before turning and striding away, taking his sword with him. The sound of the motorbike starting had her closing her eyes. It was going to be an extremely long night.

Not knowing what else to do, and not wanting to remain in the lounge room with the photos that were scattered across the coffee table, Aura went looking for Judy. She found her in the kitchen, cleaning up. Colin was nowhere in sight. The bow and quiver were also no longer on the table.

After helping Judy in the kitchen, Aura wandered

around aimlessly. When darkness fell something like an itch could be felt in her demon mark. Scratching at it didn't help. She rubbed at it, stopping and staring at the mark. That was what Riley had done the first day she'd met him. When the kangaroos had been on the road. The kangaroos that hadn't moved even though they'd driven right up to them. Had that been something to do with demons? She rubbed her wrist again. Demons were in the area.

She strode to the front door, looking outside. Movement caught her attention and she turned on the verandah light. Feud stood at the foot of the stairs. It looked like she wouldn't need to ring him after all. Seeing the flicker of flames in his eyes she swallowed hard wishing she could have rung him instead of facing him. The sensation in her demon mark increased.

"Where is the hunter?"

Aura slipped through the door, closing it carefully so it didn't make a noise. "I want my aunt."

"Do you think I care? Where is the hunter?"

Aura drew out the bloodstained cloth. "I'm willing to make a trade."

"What makes you think you have something I want?"

"Riley was injured earlier. During the fight. Not

bad. I offered to tend his wound. This is his blood. He was bragging he could leave here and you wouldn't be able to find him because you had no way of tracking him down."

Feud growled, trying to take a step forward. He was unable to come any closer. "How about I trade you your life for that cloth?"

"I want you to bring Zinnia Redding and everything that belongs to her here one hour before daybreak. You will return her to me and leave both of us unharmed and I'll give you Riley's blood. If you don't…" She let her voice trail off as she put the cloth back into her pocket.

"Where is the hunter? Why isn't he out here?"

She shrugged. "I don't know. He went out on that stupid motorbike. Judy told him it doesn't run right. Colin argued that it does. I guess he listened to the wrong one."

"Where did he go?"

She shrugged again. "He didn't say. And why would he? I only met him yesterday."

Feud grinned. A predatory one that had Aura taking a step backwards. "You would betray him?"

"I don't know him. Why would I be loyal to someone I don't know? Now my aunt is a different matter. Do we have a deal?"

He didn't answer immediately. "I will think on it." Turning, he strode away, disappearing into the darkness.

Chapter Fourteen

She stared after him. Did that mean they didn't have a deal? She automatically went to rub her demon mark again, but realised it wasn't necessary. Feud had well and truly left.

"Come inside. Don't you go letting his mind games get to you." Judy held the screen door open.

Aura followed her to the kitchen where dinner was served. She started to pull the chair out from the table, when an earlier conversation returned to her.

"Are you okay, love?" Judy asked.

Aura sat heavily in the seat, her gaze drawn to her demon mark. Riley had told her she'd be safe from Havoc tracking her down if she didn't keep banishing demons. Was her mark significant enough to catch their attention? It was certainly capable of letting her know when Feud was in the area. "How did you learn about hunters and demons?"

"They learned about us," Colin grumbled.

"What do you mean?"

"It was Emily," Judy said. "She has premonitions. She was the one that brought the hunters here. Her and the other one couldn't stay. After they'd been in the area for a few days they figured out we were the ones the demons were coming after and approached us."

"It was a week," Colin said. "It took them a week to learn we were the ones that needed help."

Judy frowned. "Are you sure? I thought it was only a few days."

Aura didn't bother listening to their mild argument. She absently ate her dinner, her gaze continually drawn to the demon mark. There wasn't anything she could do about it now. No matter the consequences, she wasn't about to sit back and wait for someone else to save Zinnia. She'd lost count of the times her aunt had helped them out over the years. The responsible one when Hazel had led them into more trouble than either of them could handle.

She'd nearly finished eating when she found herself absently rubbing her demon mark. Placing her cutlery on the plate, she rose from the table. Was it Feud? Or another demon?

"Did you want dessert?" Judy asked. "I made a chocolate pudding."

"There's a demon out the front."

"Let me get my rifle." Colin started to rise from his seat.

Her gaze was momentarily drawn to Colin's demon mark, far smaller than hers. "No. I've got this." She forced a smile to her lips. "Why not dish up some dessert for me, I'll have it when I get back." Although she had no idea how she'd manage to eat it with the way her stomach was knotted. When Judy nodded, she strode to the front door, wondering if she should have taken a weapon with her. Like her water blaster.

Feud stood at the foot of the steps. "Curtis wishes to talk to you."

"He isn't part of the deal."

"He owns Zinnia. You want her back, then he's part of the deal."

She tried to remain calm, but the thought of someone believing they owned her aunt had panic clawing at her. "What does he want?"

Feud shrugged. "You would expect me to know the workings of a human mind?"

She was half tempted to smile at the contempt in his tone. Somehow she managed to keep the smile and her flippant reply to herself, knowing it was a need to hide her fear that had her wanting to make the comment. "I'll see him. But it will have to be here. And it will have to be tonight. I doubt I'll get another chance like this. The old couple aren't happy with me and plan to tell Riley when he gets back. I want to be gone by then. Me and my aunt."

"That might not suit Curtis' plans." Feud remained silent, his gaze not leaving her. "I'll let you know his answer."

Feud was gone before she could tell him she didn't care what did or didn't suit Curtis. A second later she was relieved Feud had left before she'd said anything. Turning, she slowly made her way to the kitchen. Halfway along the hallway she stopped, leaning against the wall, eyes closed. What did she think she was doing? Riley had warned her about making any other deals with demons. Did Curtis count? She had a bad feeling he did. Images raced through her mind and she fought against giving into the panic that threatened to swamp her. Focusing on slowing her breathing she forced all the blood soaked images from her mind.

Opening her eyes, she pushed away from the wall, slowly continuing to the kitchen. She remained at the end of the hallway, watching Colin and Judy talking about plans for the farm. For when the demons were gone. They didn't notice her.

"Then when it's all back to normal, we'll invite the boys home with their families. It didn't feel right telling them not to come here for Christmas like they always do," Judy said.

Colin reached across the table and patted his wife's hand. "We'll weather this, Jude. We've survived worse."

"Our first born." Judy's voice was barely loud enough to carry to the hallway. "He was so perfect. I should have known something was wrong when he didn't cry, when they tried to take him away before I held him."

"All this has me thinking about him too." Colin patted her hand again. "We're not going to let that lot take our home from us. It's for our boys when we're gone. It's their home too."

Aura backed away, not wanting to intrude. She stumbled over her bag she'd left in the hallway earlier.

"Everything okay, love?" Judy called out.

"Ahh, yeah. I better put my bag in my room so I don't trip over it again." She picked it up.

"Your dessert is ready."

Once her bag was in her room, she joined them at the table, unable to meet their gazes. Eating the pudding, even with her stomached knotted, was preferable to looking at either of them. All this time she'd thought only of her family and how to save them. Then she'd worried about Riley. Not once had she really thought about everyone else who was involved in the situation. Hadn't thought about those who had borne more than enough and shouldn't have to go through this too.

"What did he have to say?" Judy asked.

"Is he going to-"

Judy hushed Colin. "Don't hound the girl."

"Curtis wants to speak to me." When neither of them spoke, Aura looked up to find both had horrified expressions.

"Don't meet him. He's human," Judy said.

"I don't want him on my property," Colin grumbled.

She wasn't about to let Curtis anywhere near either of them. "Can I borrow your rifle, Colin?"

"No one uses my sporterized Swedish Mauser except me. Not even my boys. I have a twenty-two they use. Can you shoot a rifle?"

She shrugged. "I've fired a rifle a few times."

"Can you hit what you're aiming at?"

"Not well."

Colin rose to his feet. "No. You can't borrow a

rifle. You're likely to shoot your foot off. Fool girl." He headed down the hallway.

"Where's he going?" Aura glanced down the hallway several times.

Judy began to clear the table. "Your aunt wouldn't want you to put yourself in harm's way for her."

A wry smile formed. Judy might be right, but that didn't change anything. "She's family."

Judy stopped, halfway back from the sink. She wiped her hands on the dishcloth she carried. "It makes a fool of all of us. These ties we make." She nodded towards the hallway. "Go on. He's probably sitting on the verandah with that rifle of his."

The meaning of the words didn't sink in immediately and Aura remained at the table as Judy started to wipe it over. "Oh. Okay." She stopped in Riley's room, grabbing three vials of holy water off his duchess. She noticed the throwing daggers she'd left on the table earlier were now on the duchess too. Her hand hovered over one of them. She had nowhere to keep it and she was probably better off not holding a weapon out when she met with them.

Feeling the arrival of demons in the area, she rubbed her demon mark, taking a deep breath before she strode to the front of the house, not about to leave Colin to face them alone. Feud stood at the bottom of the stairs on one side of a man, a woman on the other side of the man. She recognised him instantly from the photos. It was Curtis.

Colin pointed the rifle at Curtis, rising from his seat. "Don't come any closer. She can hear you fine from there. I don't want you on my property and as much as I don't like what she's doing I'm not about to send her out there to talk to you."

Curtis nodded, looking towards Aura. "Why not come a little closer?" He motioned her forward.

Light caught on the old fashioned, chunky ring he wore that contrasted with the modern watch that also reflected the light from the verandah. Aura blinked, the shine hitting her in the eyes. Had that been deliberate? "What do you want?"

"A little civility to start with," Curtis said.

"I wanted my aunt to leave with us this afternoon. Obviously we don't always get everything we want." She strode to the edge of the verandah, making sure she didn't stand between Curtis and Colin.

"Not so sweet when you're not on the other end of a phone call." The woman laughed, a brittle sound that drew Aura's attention.

She recognised the voice. It was the woman who'd answered both her calls to Blue Sky. The tall willowy woman was stunning with her dark hair and sculptured features. Until Aura looked into the dark eyes and caught the flicker of a flame. "You're a demon."

The brittle laugh rang out again. "You're not very bright."

"Bright enough to recognise you're not human." She faced Curtis again. "What do you want? Obviously something or you wouldn't be here."

"This place. We don't like neighbours."

Colin took a step towards Curtis at his words. "We're never leaving here."

"Surely they don't have to leave. Why can't you all pretend each other doesn't exist? You stay off their property and they stay off yours," Aura said.

"You think we should let this scum live next door to us?" Colin gestured towards Curtis with a dip of his rifle.

She shrugged. "There are always alternatives if you're willing to figure them out." Movement caught her attention and she saw a demon behind Curtis, nearly completely hidden by him. A painfully thin and angular demon with a grey cast to his skin. He shifted slightly, disappearing behind Curtis.

"I think," Curtis said slowly, tapping a finger against his chin. "Yes, I think we should make this a little more interesting. The hunter's blood and you for your aunt and all her belongings."

Aura's breath froze and she felt light headed.

"No." Colin came to the edge of the verandah. "Get off my property now. All of you."

She couldn't leave Zinnia with them. Images of the mutilated livestock came to mind. No way could she leave Zinnia behind. "Spell it out. What exactly do you mean when you say you want me as part of the exchange?"

"Foolish girl," Colin snapped. "Get inside. Why should you pay for the trouble your aunt got herself into?"

Aura slowly shook her head. Zinnia was too sensible for this to have been her fault. If it had been her mum, she would have known who was to blame. "How did you talk her into coming here?"

The woman laughed. "Talk? We never bother talking them into anything."

"Quiet, De," Curtis ordered.

"Do not call me by that pathetic human name. It's bad enough I have to put up with all the cattle next door calling me that."

Curtis turned his head so he was looking directly at the woman. "I will call you what I wish, Destruction. Do you not answer to me?"

Destruction laughed, this time nothing brittle in the sound.

It caused a shiver to run through Aura and made her want to back away and hide in the house.

Destruction ran a finger down Curtis' arm. "Forty-nine more years. You want to hope you find another way to prevent me from carving you into tiny little pieces before the time is up."

Curtis lifted her hand away from him, returning his attention to Aura. "You or the land. That is the choice. You have until an hour before dawn to make the decision. We will return then with your aunt. Say no and Zinnia will be the next sacrifice." Curtis smiled, the curve of his lips not changing the shape of his eyes or the expression in them.

This time Aura did take a step back, unnerved by what she saw. He expected her to say no and was looking forward to ritualistically killing her aunt. She couldn't say anything. Could only stand there and watch them disappear into the night, her heart pounding loudly enough it momentarily drowned out all other sounds.

"We need the boy. We can't do this on our own," Colin said.

She remained where she stood, staring into the night. Her, Zinnia or the land. She didn't want to die.

And she doubted Colin would give up his land for her. Not that she blamed him. She was no one to him. This was his home. The home of his sons.

"We can't take the ute. That thing can be heard from miles away," Colin said.

"The pushbike in the shed," Judy said.

Aura slowly turned, looking through the screen door. "In the dark?"

"We've another torch you can take." Judy opened the screen door. "Hurry. We're likely to need all the time we've got."

"Is it worth it, Jude? We could go live with one of the boys. Retire like they want us to." Colin remained on the verandah. "Is it worth a couple of lives?"

Seeing his dejected figure, Aura threw her arms around him, a rush of affection washing over her. She was no one, yet he was willing to give up his land for her and a woman he'd never met. "I'll go after Riley. They're not getting your land and they're not taking our lives. He'll know what to do." She wasn't absolutely certain he would, but they had until an hour before dawn to figure it out together.

Colin patted her shoulder awkwardly. "This isn't going to lead to waterworks, is it?"

Chapter Fifteen

Aura giggled at the concern she heard in Colin's tone. She hugged his narrow frame one last time before she stepped back. "No tears. Promise."

"That's okay then," Colin grumbled.

"Foolish old man." Judy ushered them inside, patting Aura on the shoulder as she walked past.

"Where's the torch?" Aura asked.

"I'll get it, you grab some weapons." Judy nodded towards Colin. "He can get the bicycle out of the shed and check there's air in the tyres and make sure the chain won't fall off."

"Don't go telling me how to do my job," Colin muttered as he headed along the hallway. "Think I don't know what I'm doing after all these years?"

"Get a roll of duct tape too. We can attach the torch to the handlebars," Judy called after him. Her only answer was more grumbles.

While Judy and Colin did their part, Aura grabbed the water blaster, two throwing daggers and more holy water. Finding a sheathed knife, she removed the knife and tested her two daggers in it. The fit wasn't perfect, but it would do. She headed to the kitchen, stopping when Judy called out.

Judy held the front door open. "The bicycle is ready. I'm afraid we don't have one of them bicycle helmets they expect you to wear these days, but there's no cars on the roads hereabouts at this hour. Rarely see anyone on the roads during the day."

Aura hurried down the steps, taking the bicycle from Colin. It looked like it was at least thirty years old, but seemed in good shape. Hopefully it wasn't like the motorbike and less reliable than it appeared.

"You stay on the roads. Don't go thinking a shortcut will save you time. It won't," Judy said.

"Okay." Aura mounted the bicycle, resting the water blaster across the handlebars before she smiled reassuringly at them and headed down the driveway.

The circle of light cast by the torch wasn't anywhere near big enough. Every sound drew her attention and she pedalled as fast as she could, jolting and jarring along the rough driveway, turning onto the main road. She hadn't realised how many sounds there were at night. Unexplainable sounds that could be absolutely anything. She frequently glanced at her demon mark, but it gave no warning of nearby demons. Having no idea how accurate it was, she continued to scan the area searching for them.

When a demon did appear in front of her, she had a second's warning, nearly riding into him. She swerved, trying to decide if she should keep riding or turn and fight. The decision was taken from her when she hit a rock hidden in the grass at the side of the road, coming off the bicycle to land sprawled in the grass.

The demon loomed over her and she scrambled to her feet as she drew out a dagger, throwing it at him. He howled, clawing at the dagger as she backed away, the light from the torch not bright enough.

The demon threw the dagger onto the ground. "You will regret that."

Aura glanced at the water blaster that wasn't far from her. Could she reach it before the demon could stop her? "The only thing I'm likely to regret is not having a dozen throwing daggers." She dived for the water blaster, the demon landing on her as her hand closed over it. Pointing it at him, she pulled the trigger, holy water making a sizzling sound as it sprayed across the demon's face.

He drew back with a howl, wiping at his face.

Aura scrambled to her feet, spraying more holy water at him. The howls of the demon rang out in the night. She was too far from the house and not close enough to the graveyard that anyone would hear his noise and come to help. She was on her own. Something she should be accustomed to. But she'd never had to face a demon alone before.

"You will regret this when I bring more demons back to show you what happens to humans who think they can attack us."

Panic swamped her and for a second she froze as the demon turned away. He could ruin everything. "Are you that weak you need help to face a single human?"

The demon kept walking. "You'll not goad me into wasting my time on you."

Dropping the water blaster, she drew the last dagger, throwing herself at the demon, who turned at the last second. The dagger sank into his chest and she prayed aloud, the words accompanied by the demon's howls. She blocked his clawed hand, drawing the dagger back and striking him with it again. When he tried to turn away, she grabbed his arm, attacking once more.

The demon fought to escape, dragging her with

him as he staggered a metre along the edge of the road before evaporating into mist.

Not expecting him to vanish so quickly, Aura landed on the ground, face first in the long grass at the side of the road. She continued to clutch the dagger, breathing hard as she rolled onto her back, abruptly ending her prayer. She stared at the stars above her, trying to slow her breathing and convince herself to rise.

She'd fought a demon. By herself. And survived. A shiver ran through her as she relived the moments, shoving the dagger in the sheath before she stumbled to her feet. He'd obviously not been a powerful demon, but somehow she'd managed. A smile slowly formed as she gathered the other dagger, the water blaster and the bicycle. She dusted the dirt from herself, wiping the demon blood from her hand in the grass, wishing she could wash it clean.

Eyeing the water blaster, she chuckled as she used it to clean her hand. She dried her hand on her jeans, taking a deep breath as she looked around the area. She'd banished a demon. On her own. The thought kept circling around in her mind. A mixture of disbelief and amazement accompanying it. Straightening her shoulders, she got back on the bike.

Surely they could rescue Zinnia. She was starting to get the hang of this demon hunting business.

The night sounds no longer seemed so sinister as she continued to the graveyard. The light of the torch fell on Riley when she drew close.

He stood at the edge of the graveyard having watched her arrival, waiting until she was close before he spoke. "Why are you here?"

"Because you didn't want me making deals with demons." She tried not to think of the one she'd fought on the way here, not sure if she should mention it to Riley. Especially since she needed to tell him about meeting Curtis.

"What happened? I thought for sure Feud would go for the offer."

"I think he would have, but Aunt Zinnia belongs to Curtis. At least that's what he said." The thought of her aunt belonging to anyone still made her feel uncomfortable. She glanced around the area. It was impossible to see anything other than shadows. "The demons didn't find you?"

"They were here for a bit."

"What happened to them?"

Riley chuckled. "A few of them decided to return home and the rest retreated."

"Voluntarily returned home?"

"I wouldn't exactly say that." He paused. "You didn't run into any of them on the way here?"

"One."

"What happened to him?"

A smile slowly formed. "He returned home."

Riley chuckled. "I take it he didn't return voluntarily."

She shook her head.

"You're unharmed?"

"Yeah." She had a few more aches, but nothing major.

"What happened with Feud? Tell me everything."

She didn't know if she should start with the ultimatum or at the beginning and tell him everything in order. "Do they kill you first? You know, when they sacrifice you."

He gripped her arm. "What happened? Tell me."

She was glad of the shadows pressing in around them, making it easier for her to tell him what had happened. She didn't think she wanted to know what sort of emotion she would see deep in his dark brown eyes. When she finished speaking, she looked at the torch taped to the handlebars, moths flying around in front of it. Was he going to say something? She glanced at him, returning her gaze to the moths.

"We need to go back to Colin's place." He scanned the area. "There are no demons nearby. Yet."

"What are we going to do?" She didn't want to exchange herself for Zinnia, but neither did she want anything to happen to her aunt.

"We'll work it out. I'll grab the motorbike and put everything in the saddlebags so we can go."

She watched his figure move around the graveyard, eventually pushing the motorbike towards her. "What if we run into demons on the way back?" She wasn't sure if she was up to facing another demon so soon.

"I don't think we will. Or at least no major ones. I can't feel any nearby." He remained at her side, pushing the motorbike rather than leave her behind.

"Does that mean they're planning something?"

Riley chuckled. "They're demons. They're always planning something."

"Riley." She glanced towards him, annoyance in her tone. "What can we expect? And what can we do? I don't want to die."

"I can't promise you won't. I'll do everything possible to try and keep you alive, but there are no guarantees. Not with demons."

She wanted to beg him to tell her something different. "Okay. No guarantees. What can we do?"

"I need to ring my brother and find out how close he is."

"What can he do?"

"I'm thinking. I'll let you know when I've figured it out."

She started to ask him another question, closing her mouth instead. There were some things she was better off not knowing. She had more than enough vivid images capable of providing nightmares for a lifetime. It was probably a good thing he hadn't answered her before about if human sacrifices were killed before the sacrifice was made. She hadn't been able to figure out a single positive outcome. Death seemed like a possibility. No matter what decision they made. Riley's comments about major demons reminded her that the ones they planned to face were more powerful than the one she'd banished on her own.

Colin waited on the verandah for them, rising to his feet as they approached, holding his rifle. "We've had no more visitors. It's quiet out there."

Riley emptied the saddlebags, giving the tools to Colin as he walked past him. "I doubt it'll stay that way."

"Judy and I were talking. About what that man wants," Colin said.

Aura spoke before Colin could continue. "You're not exchanging your land. We're not about to give into them."

Riley opened the screen door, looking over his shoulder to Colin. "I need to ring my brother. I have to find out how far away he is from here."

Colin nodded. "I'll keep watch."

Riley inclined his head. "Thanks." He strode inside, heading straight to the lounge room and the rotary dial phone.

Aura turned off the torch and took the water blaster with her when she followed Riley. She remained beside him while he dialled the number, having left the water blaster against the wall by the doorway. She listened to Riley's side of the conversation as he explained what had happened. Curtis's demands sounded worse the more times she heard them spoken.

Riley slowly nodded. "Okay, I'll see the pair of you then."

"What is happening?" Aura asked. "Who is with him?"

"His girlfriend. Allie."

"Your brother takes his girlfriend with him when he hunts demons?" She stared at him when he nodded. "That's not very romantic."

Riley grinned. "I guess that depends on your point of view."

"What are we going to do while we wait for them?"

"Have a nap." He started to stride from the room.

She grabbed hold of his arm. "Have a nap? Are you serious? Curtis wants me to exchange myself for my aunt. Do you really think I'll be able to sleep?"

"Yes. You look tired and exhausted. Even a rest will help." He tugged his arm from her grip and captured her hand. "You need to be alert when dealing with demons."

"I suppose I could try." She didn't want anything to go wrong since they had no plan. And it seemed like there was a lot that could go wrong. She tugged her hand from his. "I suppose I should–" She made a vague gesture towards the hallway that led to the room she was staying in.

Riley captured her hand again, moving closer. "Do you want me to sit with you?"

A wry smile formed. "What are you in your spare time when you aren't hunting demons? A guardian angel?"

Riley chuckled. "I'm afraid I'm too much of a sinner for that. No human is that perfect." He walked beside her to the bedroom, nodding towards Judy who stood at the end of the hallway.

"You better not let her hand herself over." Judy pointed a warning finger at Riley.

"I'm sure I can come up with a better plan than that." Riley grinned. "Something a little more spectacular."

Judy nodded. "Make sure you do." She turned to Aura. "If you don't need anything else, I'm off to bed. That fool of a husband of mine should be in bed too. He's not as young as he once was. Neither of us are."

"I'll send him off to bed shortly. I doubt the demons will come back until it's time to make their trade. They think they've won this round," Riley said.

With another nod, Judy headed down the hallway to her room.

Aura grabbed the water blaster before she made her way down the hallway and turned on the light switch in the bedroom. "This is probably a waste of time. There's no way I'm going to manage to sleep."

"I'll wake you when my brother arrives." Riley nodded towards the bed. "Better have that rest while you can."

Chapter Sixteen

Aura moved back into the hall and watched as Riley strode towards the front door. She entered the bedroom once he'd stepped out onto the verandah. She put the daggers and water blaster on the duchess before lying down. Staring at the ceiling, she was surprised to be woken what felt like minutes later. "I slept?"

"Blake and Allie are here."

"How long did I sleep?" She sat up, glancing around the room. The light was on and the curtain drawn.

"It's two hours until dawn. We have less than an hour to come up with a plan."

She sat on the edge of the bed, trying not to yawn. "I can't believe I slept."

"They're waiting in the kitchen for us." Riley gestured towards the door.

She nodded, trying to focus. "I'll be out in a minute."

Riley looked her over, then nodded, striding from the room.

She stared at the empty doorway a moment before rising to her feet and gathering her weapons. Her hand hesitated over the water blaster. In the end, she left it on the duchess. It was pretty bulky to cart around. She stopped at the end of the hallway, her gaze roaming across the people at the table. Along with Riley were two others.

There was a young woman, who looked to be around her age, with dark hair cut in layers to fall just past her shoulders, a blood red streak curving from the crown of her head to brush her left cheek. She had high cheekbones and green eyes. The other was a young man who wore a black t-shirt that revealed a demon mark that curved all the way from his wrist to his elbow. It had been tattooed to look like barbed wire, the ink as red as the young woman's lock of hair. He had blue eyes, dark hair and a slightly scruffy look. Like him, the young woman was also dressed in black. Both her shirt and jeans.

Riley spotted her and smiled, beckoning her forward. "This is Blake and Allie."

Aura entered the kitchen and sat beside Riley. She

tried to smile, but it was impossible. There was so little time before Curtis returned. "What are we going to do? What can we do?"

"I'm going to assume you're not interested in becoming a blood sacrifice," Blake said.

She shuddered. "I'm really hoping to avoid that."

"I don't blame you." Allie gave her a sympathetic smile. "Trust me when I say it's not something you want to experience."

Realising her mouth was open, Aura closed it. "Someone tried to use you as a human sacrifice?"

"It's a long story." She reached for Blake's hand, linking her fingers through his.

"We need more information. What exactly is going on next door?" Blake asked.

"I haven't been able to get over there," Riley said. "Curtis never seems to leave."

"He won't be over there in an hour," Blake said.

"Someone needs to be here to make the exchange with Curtis," Riley said.

"We can do that," Allie said. "It makes sense that neither of you would be here. We can say Aura went next door leaving us to make the exchange so her aunt couldn't talk her out of it."

"Why would you give up Riley's blood?" Aura asked.

"We wouldn't," Blake said. "But if the item is wrapped up, how would we know what we're handing over?"

"You don't have to come next door with me," Riley said. "I can take you to the graveyard where you'll be safe until we come for you."

She was more than tempted to take him up on the offer. "No. Aunt Zinnia is my family. I'm not about to sit back and wait for everyone else to risk their lives for her. For us."

Blake met her gaze. "Make sure you're up to this. Or you will be putting our lives at even greater risk."

"She's up to it," Riley said.

His words surprised her. There'd been no hesitation. "Why would Riley be with me if I'm going next door to offer myself up in exchange?"

"I wouldn't. You'd be entering on your own," Riley said. "Can you manage that?"

"Where will you be?" Aura asked.

"Following you." Riley grinned. "You didn't think I was going to let you keep all the excitement to yourself, did you?"

"How many will be next door when Curtis is over here?" Aura asked.

Riley shrugged. "We're going in blind. We have

no idea who or what is over there. Are you sure you want to do this?"

She tried to say yes, but all she could do was nod. She didn't want to go at all. Her gaze moved to Blake and Allie. "Thank you for helping."

Blake shrugged. "It's our job."

Allie grinned. "Yep, it's our job. Although it's probably going to be a little hard to do my job for a while since I'm going to be grounded again."

Riley chuckled. "You snuck away?"

Allie raised her chin. "I wasn't about to let Blake do this on his own. I told all of you that nothing would change. No matter what I do, they're going to keep treating me like a little kid. I wish I could afford to move out of home."

Riley rose from the chair. "It'll probably come to that eventually." He turned to Aura. "I'll get a couple of vials of holy water for you."

Aura stood up as well. "I was thinking of taking the water blaster."

Riley shook his head. "It's too obvious. You're meant to be handing yourself in, not waging war."

"What about my throwing daggers? Do I get to take them?"

"Yeah, it's unlikely that you'd go in completely unarmed." Riley turned to Blake. "Don't let Zinnia go anywhere and keep Curtis and his demons here for as long as possible."

"We will." Blake held out his left hand, clasping hand to forearm, wrist to wrist with Riley.

"Tell them you came here looking for me and demand to know if they've done something to me." Riley released his brother's arm and stepped back.

Aura followed Riley to his bedroom, taking the vials of holy water and tucking them into the pockets of her jeans. "When are we leaving?"

Riley checked the time. "Very soon. Are you sure you want to do this? Last chance to say no."

"I'm not about to sit around waiting to become a sacrifice. Or let that happen to Aunt Zinnia."

Riley gathered his weapons. Sword at his back in a scabbard, a quiver of arrows hanging from his belt at his side, various vials of holy water stashed in pockets and a dagger in his boot, his bow in his left hand. "We're going to walk over. We don't want them to notice us coming."

"What about when it's time to leave? How will we get away without transport?"

"That will be the tricky part." Riley grinned. "You still coming?"

"I thought you'd already given me my last chance to decline."

Riley chuckled. "Let's go then." He led the way to the front door, holding the screen open for her.

She hesitated on the last step leading off the verandah. The moment she stepped onto the ground she was no longer safe from demons. Not that being on the verandah was all that safe. Humans could enter the house. She placed her foot on the ground, checking her surroundings before following Riley in the direction of Blue Sky.

Riley carried a small torch, the feeble light doing very little to show the way. "We'll head around to the back of the building and remain at a distance until they leave."

"How will we know they've left?"

"You'll know."

They remained silent, needing to go through a couple of barbed wire fences, not talking until they were in position. They overlooked the back of the house, but were far enough away that the demons shouldn't notice them. Aura rubbed her left wrist. "How long does this work? The ability to feel demons through the demon mark."

"Always."

"Oh." She tried not to rub her wrist. It was impossible to stop. Then the sensation lessened. "They're leaving?"

"At least Feud is. He's the demon with the most power here. Although Curtis feels like he might have more power than Feud." Riley held the torch near the end, his hand preventing most of the light from escaping. "Stay close and try not to talk."

She nodded, moving closer to him, trying to see where she walked. It was an impossible task, made more so by the deeper shadows when they came closer to the building. They moved along the back of the building, looking for a way in. Several of the windows they looked through had people sleeping in the rooms. They kept looking, finding an empty room at the corner of the sprawling house.

Pushing the curtain further across the rod, Aura climbed inside, Riley having run a knife through the screen at the window. Enough light came in the window from the torch Riley held, no longer blocking most of the light, that she could see the carpet that had once been on the floor was rolled up and along one side of the room, leaving behind an unvarnished timber floor. She crossed the room to try the door. It was locked so she took out her phone and used the light of it to see the room better. She froze, drawing in a sharp breath.

Riley entered through the window, coming to a

stop beside her, shining the torch around the room. "A Pentagram. This isn't good."

Aura moved closer, her gaze fixed on the symbol etched into the timber floor, the markings stained dark in some spots. It took her a few seconds to realise it was dried blood. "What does it do?"

"A human can enter and leave at will. To a demon, it's a trap. They're probably summoning them into this circle and not letting them out of it until they reach an agreement."

Before Aura could ask another question, the door opened and a demon entered the room. The painfully thin and angular demon that had hidden behind Curtis. In the light from the phone his skin looked more grey than it had from the light of the verandah. She took a step backwards.

"He said it was a trap. That you would not turn yourself over to us," the demon said.

Riley grabbed her by the arm, tugging her towards the pentagram. "Who are you and what do you want?"

"He's the demon who was hiding behind Curtis," Aura said.

"I hide behind no one. It is where he requested I be. At his shoulder. Ready to serve his every whim."

Aura was surprised at the bitterness she heard in the demon's voice. "You don't like him?"

"Curtis probably trapped him," Riley said.

"That knowledge will do you no good, hunter. I have lost count of the amount of hunters Curtis has vanquished over the years."

"Why isn't he doing anything?" Aura whispered.

"Curiosity, maybe?"

"How can we win against him?" Aura asked.

The demon grinned, no humour in it. "By getting past me. Think you're capable?"

"Do you serve him through choice or have no choice other than to serve him?" Riley asked.

The demon came closer, his feet stopping millimetres from the pentagram. "That knowledge will not help you defeat me. Nor will your prayers help you banish me."

"You're bound?" Riley asked.

The demon looked at the floor. "You cannot stay in there forever. Eventually Curtis will return and he can come after you himself instead of making me the errand boy."

"What object are you bound to?" Riley asked.

"Although I suppose your unwillingness to face me will only ensure you're here when Curtis returns. He will be pleased to learn I have you cornered." Again he grinned. "Both of you."

It struck Aura like a flash of light. "The ring. That old fashioned ring Curtis wears."

Riley slowly nodded. "A ring is a common choice. It's harder to take a ring from someone than most other pieces of jewellery."

"You think you're the first to try and take me from him?" the demon asked.

"There is a difference between us and others who have tried to take the ring," Riley said.

"And what would that difference be?" the demon asked.

"What is the name they call you by?" Riley asked.

"If I give you this information will you give me the answer?"

Riley nodded.

Aura wanted to demand what Riley was doing. They should be running. If the demon was to be believed, Curtis would be here soon and they'd both be caught.

"Bane. Bane of his existence." Once again the demon's voice was bitter. "Yet he would not be alive without me."

"The difference between me and others who have

gone after the ring is that I don't want to keep you bound to it," Riley said.

"Why would I believe you?" Bane demanded.

"I'm a hunter. What use have I for a bound demon?"

"You're trying to tell me you'd set me free to do as I wish in this world."

Aura felt as sceptical as the demon sounded. Surely Riley wouldn't let him go free. Bane was a demon.

"I would set you free, but if you used your freedom to harm humans, I would come after you. I would track you down and return you to hell," Riley stated.

"Another five minutes and it won't matter," Bane said. "He has left the others to deal with those next door. He's coming after the two of you. There's nothing to keep me from protecting him." Once more Bane's gaze was drawn to the floor. "Such as a trap."

Chapter Seventeen

Aura stared at Bane. Had he told them to trap him? She glanced at Riley. His attention remained on the demon.

Riley held out a hand, keeping it within the pentagram. "Are you strong enough to draw me from this trap?"

Bane held out his hand, staying outside the edge of the pentagram. "Why not find out? Or will you cheat and have your companion help?"

Aura was certain of it. He was telling them to trap him and how to do it. She tensed, ready to help Riley if he needed her.

Riley extended his hand past the edge of the pentagram.

Bane grabbed hold of Riley's hand and started to drag him out. Aura grabbed Bane's arm and pulled him into the pentagram with them. He fought them, knocking Aura to the ground so she fell outside the pentagram. She staggered to her feet, still clutching her phone and shining it around to see what was happening. She saw Riley flung from Bane, landing slumped on the floor across the room.

The door to the room opened and the light was switched on. Curtis strode inside. He glared at Bane. "I will deal with you later."

Riley rose to his feet, putting an arrow to his bow, the torch left lying on the floor. "Day is nearly here. Your more powerful demons are about to desert you."

"You think I am powerless without demons?" Curtis slowly walked towards Riley.

Aura looked between the three occupants of the room, not sure what to do. The last thing she wanted to do was catch the attention of Curtis.

"I have seen and done more than you will ever have the chance to do." Curtis' attention remained on Riley. He held a hand out towards Bane. "A sword. Now."

A sword appeared in Bane's hand and he slid it across the floor to Curtis.

Picking up the sword, Curtis smiled. "Even weak, pathetic and trapped in a pentagram, my demon is of some use. And I have only to call the others to me and they will be here. What can you do against that, hunter?"

Riley grinned. "Pray." He released the arrow.

Curtis struck the arrow from the air with his sword, laughing. "You think that will help?"

"I guess we'll have to wait and see." Riley fired at Curtis again, glancing at Aura when Curtis again struck out at the arrow.

Aura frowned. What was he trying to tell her? Her gaze was drawn to Curtis' other hand. The one he wore the ring on. As he swung the sword at another arrow his hand splayed open before becoming a fist again. She looked from the ring to Riley and back again. Surely he didn't expect her to try and get the ring.

"You'll eventually run out of arrows," Curtis said.

She slipped her phone into her pocket, taking a deep breath. She dreaded to think what would happen once Riley had fired his last arrow. She took a step towards Curtis, his back to her. A glance at Bane showed he was smiling, his gaze firmly on her. Would he say something to Curtis? She had no idea. What she did know was that the floor around Curtis was becoming littered with arrows. Most of them broken.

"When there are no arrows left, I have my sword." Riley fired another arrow at Curtis.

Directly behind Curtis, she crouched, her gaze fixed on his hand. Holding her breath, she reached for him. His hand splayed and she grabbed the ring, sliding it off his finger, surprised it came off so easily.

Curtis spun to face her, raising his sword.

She scrambled away, landing sprawled on the floor.

"Put it on." Riley tackled Curtis. "Aura, put it on."

She slipped the ring over a finger, curling her hand into a fist to keep it from falling off.

"No!" Bane howled, trying to escape the pentagram. "Set me free."

Riley blocked a punch from Curtis. "Run, Aura. Don't stop until you've returned to Colin and Judy's. Not for anything."

She stumbled to her feet. "You–"

Curtis' fist connected with Riley's jaw. "If you run I will make you beg for death. But I will not allow you that release."

"Trust me. Run." Riley blocked another punch, getting in one of his own.

She had no idea what to do. Bane continued to scream at her and Riley fought against Curtis. How could she desert him?

"Aura! Go to Blake."

Nodding, she ran to the window and climbed outside. She'd forgotten about the other hunters. Help. That's what they needed. She'd bring back help. The land was filled with early morning light, the heat already starting. She ran towards Colin and Judy's farm, her hand kept in a tight fist so she didn't lose the ring.

As she left Blue Sky behind, she slowed, unable to maintain her initial speed. She glanced over her shoulder. No one followed. The thought of Riley left behind made her want to run faster, but she couldn't. Why had they walked over? They could have brought the bicycle and come by the road. And what did Riley plan to do with the ring? Surely he wasn't going to keep the demon.

She was forced to come to a stop a couple of times to clamber through barbed wire fences. Each time she looked over her shoulder, but no one followed. Not even Riley. She stumbled. Should she have left him behind? What if the other hunters couldn't get back in time to help him? Could he last at least twenty minutes before someone could arrive at Blue Sky? That seemed like a really long time when you were fighting for your life.

The house came into view and she slowed as she saw Blake and Allie out the front fighting

Destruction. Colin remained on the verandah, his rifle pointed in the direction of the rapidly moving figures. Her heart plummeted. How were they meant to help when they had a demon of their own to deal with?

"Aura." Zinnia came running out of the house, prevented from leaving the verandah by Colin.

Even the sight of her aunt didn't make her feel any better. She should have stayed. Shouldn't have deserted Riley. She stopped at the bottom of the steps, her back to the house. "Riley is fighting Curtis on his own."

Destruction glanced at Aura. She took a second look. "You have his ring." She tried to head towards Aura.

Behind her, Aura could hear Zinnia argue with Colin to let her go. "You have to help him." She looked from Allie to Blake. "You have to go after him."

"How was he?" Blake asked.

"Did Curtis have help?" Allie prevented Destruction from coming closer to the house.

"Bane was trapped by a pentagram and Curtis was alone, but that could change. It might already have changed." Aura wanted to demand why they weren't more worried.

"It already has changed."

At the familiar voice, Aura looked in the direction of Blue Sky. Riley ran towards her, grinning, a bruise on his jaw. For a few seconds she couldn't believe what she was seeing. Then she ran towards him, throwing her arms around his neck and drawing him close, her lips meeting his.

Riley slid one arm around her waist, the bow in his other hand. He returned her kiss, eventually drawing back. "You have the ring?"

She nodded, her gaze roaming his face.

"Good." He looked past her to Destruction. "Once we get rid of her, we have some planning to do." Letting go of Aura, he drew his sword and strode towards the fight, the bow in his left hand.

She wanted to drag him back. Wanted to tell him he'd faced enough danger for the day. But doubted he'd listen. Not with the enthusiastic way he joined the fight. On the verandah Zinnia and Colin continued to argue. She wasn't tempted to join her aunt. Drawing one of the daggers, she waited for an opening, throwing it at Destruction.

The demon howled, turning to face her, trying to get past the demon hunters to attack her. "You will regret that." With a snarl, Destruction spun away, escaping from the hunters, racing down the driveway.

"Let her go," Blake ordered when Allie and Riley went to follow. "We have other things to focus on." He strode towards the house.

Aura stared in the direction Destruction had taken. "What if she tells Feud that I wouldn't be disloyal to you?" She turned to Riley. When she'd thrown herself at him, she hadn't thought about their earlier plans.

Riley sheathed his sword. "I doubt she'll have the chance. As long as I'm not in the area Feud won't wait around to talk to anyone. He'll come straight after me." He nodded towards the house. "Don't worry. We'll figure it out."

Colin stepped out of the way, him and Zinnia falling silent. Zinnia grabbed Aura's arm as she stepped onto the verandah. "My tie to the demons has been broken. We're leaving. Get your things and let's go. My car is parked at the end of the driveway."

Aura shook her head, pulling her arm out of Zinnia's grip. "I'm not going. Not until Colin and Judy's farm is safe and the rest of the people of Blue Sky are free."

"This has nothing to do with us. Don't you have enough problems looking after your mother without taking on someone else's?"

"What happened to Mum next door? Why didn't she throw up blood like you?" Aura glanced at Riley who came to stand next to her, having left his bow by the door. She gave him a smile before she returned her attention to Zinnia.

Zinnia slowly shook her head. "It was probably one of the few times in her life when being ditzy has been a benefit. They kept trying to get Hazel to drink, but she didn't drink enough to sedate her so they could draw blood from her. I wanted to warn her, but they ordered me not to say anything. Just like I wanted to warn you in the car yesterday. They planned to question her before they let her know what they are and what is going on."

"Why didn't they take the blood from her?" Aura asked.

"A few times they tried to take it by accidentally on purpose hurting her, but Hazel often moves erratically. A pretty butterfly flitting from place to place. Impossible to predict. You cannot imagine how hard it was to be trapped next door, knowing what was going on and unable to do anything about it." Zinnia rested her hands on Aura's shoulders. "We can't stay here. I don't want that for you."

"I'll need the ring before you leave," Riley said.

Aura pulled away from Zinnia to face Riley,

noticing that everyone else had gone inside, leaving only the three of them on the verandah. "What are you going to do with it?"

"Set him free. Once I deal with Feud."

Bane stepped into view at the end of the verandah, standing as close to the house as he could. "It wasn't a trick?"

Aura glanced at her demon mark. "Why didn't I sense him with how close he is?"

"I felt him there, but we aren't discussing any secrets. You wouldn't have felt him because he has so little power he barely exists," Riley said.

"Do you want to find out what it is like not to exist?" Bane demanded.

Riley grinned. "You're not encouraging me to follow through with the plan to set you free."

"I can't go against Curtis. He'll always be my master no matter who wears the ring, which is why he sent me after you. So be careful what you order me to do while you wear that ring." Bane nodded towards Aura's hand.

"Order?" Aura looked from the ring to Bane. Had her mum been right? "Like genie wishes?"

"I am no ifrit," Bane snarled.

Aura looked to Riley, not sure how she'd offended Bane. Although judging by Riley's grin, he was amused. She turned back to Bane. "What can you do then?"

Riley captured her hands, facing her, his grin gone. "No. No dealings with demons. You will not make a bargain with him or have him help us in any way. Demon gratitude can be worse than their animosity."

"It doesn't matter," Zinnia said. "We're leaving."

Aura shook her head, the words she started to speak interrupted by Blake coming to the door.

"You need to get on the road soon if you want to be well away from here before the sun sets and Feud comes after you."

Aura's gaze was drawn to Blake's arm. What had he faced to gain such a long demon mark? She glanced at her own that had grown another millimetre. It had to be pretty major considering he looked to be only a few years older than her. She turned to Riley. "You're not going alone."

"Blake and Allie are going to stay here and guard Colin and Judy," Riley said.

She shook her head. "You're not facing Feud alone." There was no way Riley could beat Feud. The demon was taller and stronger than him.

"You're not going with him," Zinnia said.

"Aren't I?" Aura smiled at Zinnia's expression. The same exasperated one she regularly saw when Zinnia was dealing with her mum. "There's nothing you can say that will change my mind." She'd already deserted Riley once. She wasn't going to do it a second time. No matter what he said.

"What about your mother? Who is going to keep her out of trouble?" Zinnia asked.

Aura moved closer to Zinnia. "You are. I need you to stop Mum from returning. The hunters can't keep her out of trouble forever. And we really don't want her back here messing with demons."

"Do you think she'll leave you here? She is your mother after all."

Aura nodded. "If she's distracted."

Zinnia started to argue. "Who am I kidding? She loves you dearly, but she's hopeless. You're probably more capable than the pair of us put together. Which isn't saying much when you take Hazel into account."

Grinning, she threw her arms around Zinnia. "I love you, Aunt Zin."

Zinnia returned the hug. "I love you too, Aura. Remember you're strong. Though I'm not sure how that came about."

She drew back to meet Zinnia's gaze. "I guess I took after you instead of Mum."

"God forbid!"

Aura chuckled. "Absolutely not. There's nothing wrong with you."

"Try not to go rushing headlong into danger," Zinnia said.

Riley stepped closer to Aura. "Are you sure you want to do this? If that demon mark gets much longer you will be noticed by them."

She looked from the mark to Riley, Zinnia and Blake before her gaze returned to her wrist. Images rushed through her mind. The ritualistic slaughtered livestock, Zinnia throwing up blood, the flicker of flames in Feud's eyes, the kangaroos that blocked their way, fighting beside Colin and banishing a demon on her own. There was no way she could walk away and forget all of this existed. Smiling, her gaze met Riley's. "How do you become a hunter?" Laughter drew her attention and she saw Allie had come to the door to stand next to Blake.

"You're either born to it or are dragged into it," Allie said.

Riley grinned. "That pretty much sums it up." He looked to Zinnia. "We'll escort you to your car so you can leave before any other demons decide to turn up." He held out his hand to Aura. "Can I have that ring now?"

"You're certain you're going to set him free?"

"We only hunt down demons that cause harm to humans and we don't believe in slavery." He continued to hold out his hand.

She removed the ring and placed it in his hand. "Good. I'm glad we didn't lie to him." Even though he was a demon, tricking him into helping them would have felt wrong. Like something a demon would have done. And she didn't want to be anything like a demon.

Riley slipped the ring onto his finger, glancing at his brother. "We'll be back shortly." He grinned. "I don't suppose you can ask Judy to have breakfast ready."

Aura glanced at Bane who kept pace with them as they walked along the driveway. She might not have wanted to trick him, but that didn't mean she trusted him. Trying not to keep glancing at him, she spoke to Zinnia. "Tell Mum I'll be home soon."

"I keep thinking this is a bad idea. That I should stay here with you," Zinnia said.

"You know someone is going to have to keep Mum out of trouble." Aura smiled. "I'd rather not have to deal with more messes the moment I get home."

Zinnia stopped by her car and turned to face them.

"Be very careful, Aura. Both your mother and I would be devastated if anything happened to you."

After a glance at the second vehicle parked at the start of the driveway, Aura hugged Zinnia again. "I've been taking care of myself for years. I'm more than capable of doing this." At least she hoped she was.

Zinnia patted her on the back before she let her go. "I know. Otherwise there's no way in hell I'd leave you here alone." Zinnia held Aura's gaze a moment longer before glancing at the other two. "Ring me if you need me."

Chapter Eighteen

Aura slipped an arm around Riley's waist as she watched her aunt go, waving at the disappearing vehicle. The relief she'd expected to feel at getting her aunt away didn't arrive. There were obviously too many other things to worry about. "What now?" She glanced at Riley, keeping her arm around him.

Riley had his arm around her shoulders. "We talk to Blake and Allie." His gaze went to the demon. "And you will not return to the house with us. We can't trust you with our plans."

"The only plan I care about is the one to set me free. When will that happen?" Bane asked.

"I can't risk setting you free until after I've done something about Feud," Riley said.

"You talk as if it's possible to set me free now," Bane said. "Have you everything you need to release me? Including the blood of the one who bound me to the ring."

"I know what is needed to break the bond," Riley said.

"I didn't ask if you knew what was needed." Bane took a step towards Riley, the flicker of flames appearing momentarily in his eyes. "I want to know if you have everything needed. Curtis' blood, holy water and Holy Chrism oil."

"And if I do?" Riley asked.

"Then I must prevent you from breaking the bond," Bane said.

Riley inclined his head. "That is what I thought." He grinned. "Do you think hunters wander around with Holy Chrism oil on them?"

"When you have all the necessary ingredients I will need to stop you from using them," Bane said.

"Was that a warning or a threat?" Aura asked.

"It would have to be a threat since I could not give a warning," Bane said. "That would be going against my real master's wishes."

"You need to wait here while I talk to my brother," Riley said.

"I can give you half an hour. I will not be able to leave you out of my sight longer than that. I cannot risk you doing something to the ring," Bane said.

Riley nodded, keeping his arm around Aura as he headed back towards the house. "Let's hope half an hour is long enough."

Aura waited until they were far enough away from Bane that he was unlikely to hear her before she spoke. "Whose car is that at the end of the driveway?"

"I guess it's the one they brought for me since there's a four-wheel-drive parked up near the house."

Her gaze was drawn to the bruise on his jaw. "I shouldn't have left you behind."

"If you're going to start thinking like that, you won't be coming with me."

"But–"

"I'm serious, Aura. The ring needed to be taken to safety. Part of being a hunter means you have to follow the orders of whoever is leader of the team at the time."

Laughter drew Aura's attention to where Blake and Allie sat on the top step of the verandah. Both were laughing. She looked between them and Riley. "I'm missing something, aren't I?"

Allie rose to her feet. "Hunters are a pretty independent lot. They work in teams and frequently ignore orders." She grinned, looking at Riley. "Isn't that right, Riley?"

Riley returned her grin. "How about you tell me, Allie?"

Blake chuckled. "You can't win this one, Allie Cat."

Riley headed up the steps and they got out of his way. "We have less than half an hour before Bane will be listening in again." He led the way to the kitchen table.

Judy was serving breakfast. "I was about to send Colin to let you know food is ready."

After setting aside weapons, they all sat around the table. Colin finished wiping dust from the extra chairs he'd brought in from the shed. Blake slid a ring across the table to Riley, saying nothing.

Riley stared at it for a moment. "Gran suggested this?"

"She doesn't want you to keep him," Blake said between mouthfuls.

"It's about the only way to stop him from coming after you," Allie said.

Finishing her mouthful, Aura gestured towards the simple gold ring that remained on the table. "How is that any different to Curtis binding Bane to a ring? I thought you said you don't believe in slavery."

"No one will have access to this ring. It will be put somewhere safe. There's a difference between slavery and incarceration." Blake gestured towards the ring. "That is a last resort. When no other option is possible."

"Is there anywhere safe from demons?" Aura asked.

"Any place that is consecrated," Blake said.

Aura's gaze remained on the ring for a moment, thinking about all the problems Curtis had caused by having a demon at his beck and call. "That won't keep it safe from humans."

Riley covered her hand with his, smiling at her. "There are consecrated places that it's impossible for the average human to gain access to."

"Like where?" Aura asked.

"The Vatican," Colin said.

Aura looked from Colin to Riley. "Is that where the ring will be stored?"

Riley shrugged. "It wouldn't be up to us, but yes, a place like that."

"Who would it be up to?" Aura asked.

"Gran," Riley and Blake said at the same time.

Allie set down her cutlery, finished her food. "You can trust Gran. I mightn't always agree with her, but she's fiercely protective of her family and has spent her life fighting demons. Her parents were the first demon hunters in Australia."

Riley picked up the ring, turning it in his fingers,

light catching on its surface. "This won't keep Curtis from summoning other demons. It will only take one off the board."

"One is a start." Blake nodded to the ring Riley wore. "After which we'll take a second one off the board."

"I need the rest of the ingredients," Riley said.

Blake took a small vial of oil from his pocket and tossed it across the table to Riley who caught it and slipped it in a pocket.

Aura nearly asked what it was, but worried a demon might be listening she remained silent. How long did her demon mark need to be before she could tell if the weak ones were around?

Riley rose from the table. "I'll pack some gear and we'll head to a suitable location to trap Feud."

"Return the moment he's dealt with," Blake said. "We don't want to give Curtis the chance to make plans to disappear. Losing his demon might be enough to send him running."

"He has Destruction. She has to answer to him for another forty-nine years." Aura frowned, trying to remember everything Destruction had said about their alliance. "She's not happy about it and plans to carve him into little pieces when the forty-nine years are up unless he finds a way to prevent her."

Riley stared at Aura for a moment. "I wonder if Bane knows the story behind that alliance."

"Don't go doing anything stupid, Ry," Blake warned.

Riley grinned. "Me? Do something stupid?" He laughed. "You worry too much, brother." He strode from the kitchen.

Aura stared after him. "Will he? Do something stupid, that is."

Blake shrugged. "I guess we'll see."

That wasn't what she wanted to hear. Before she could ask another question, Riley returned.

"You have to take Colin and Judy and get out of here, Blake. Curtis is rallying the residents of Blue Sky. He's sending the residents to take both of them alive. He plans to trade them for the ring. We have fifteen minutes to leave."

"How do you know that?" Aura asked.

"Because Bane was gloating." Riley grinned. "And it was gloating since it's impossible for him to give a warning."

"We're not leaving our home," Colin stated.

"Temporarily," Blake said. "A day or two at the most. If you're not here, they won't do anything. That's the way it works. They'll follow his orders to the letter. If you're here, they'll do anything to capture you, including destroying your home."

"Get moving, you old fool." Judy shooed Colin from the kitchen. "Grab your wallet and lock your rifle away. It's past time we caught up with our boys." She turned to Blake. "Can you drop us in town? We can catch a bus to Brisbane."

Blake nodded. "Did you want us to arrange for someone to pick you up?"

Judy shook her head, heading towards the hallway. "We'll ring our eldest when we arrive." She glanced over her shoulder. "Don't stand around doing nothing or you'll be wearing the clothes you stand in for the next week."

Aura grinned when Colin followed his wife, grumbling about how bossy she was. "I'll see if they need any help."

Riley captured her arm, when she started to walk past him. "You'll only get in the way. If you want to help, we need to take all my weapons out to Blake's vehicle. I'm not about to leave them lying around for anyone to pick up."

They were ready in less than ten minutes, Blake dropping them at the end of the driveway before heading towards town. They kept a handful of weapons and their suitcases, which they put in the car that had been brought for Riley to use. Bane got in the back seat, smiling when Riley looked at him. With a shake of his head, Riley sat in the driver's seat and, the moment Aura was buckled up, headed in the opposite direction to which Blake had taken.

"Why are we going this way?" She glanced over her shoulder at Bane, uncomfortable to have a demon sitting behind her.

"It's a good direction to take," Riley said.

"You can discuss your plans. I can't go far from the ring," Bane said. "A couple of kilometres at the most. It used to be less, but Curtis improved the binding. With the help of more powerful demons."

Aura turned in her seat, frowning as she looked at Bane. "That bothers you?"

"Which in particular? I mentioned several topics."

"More powerful demons. Are you scared of them?"

Flames leapt in Bane's eyes. "That should have been me. I should be more powerful. I have walked this earth for a hundred and fifty years. My power should be great instead of worn away by a human."

She nearly drew back from the anger in his voice, the scent of smoke faint on the air. "Smoke? Is something-"

Riley interrupted her. "Demons smell of smoke, fire or sulphur. Or something similar."

"I couldn't smell it before," Aura said.

Riley grinned. "You're only smelling it now because Bane is a little upset. He's not strong enough to have a stronger scent."

"I am more powerful than you, hunter." Bane spoke through clenched teeth, flames dancing in his eyes.

Aura looked from Riley to Bane, wondering if this was one of those moments Blake had been referring to. "You're not planning on doing anything stupid, are you?"

Riley laughed. "You shouldn't listen to my brother. Older siblings are meant to worry about the younger ones. It's in the job description."

"I wouldn't know. I don't have any siblings." Thoughts of her mum came to mind. Well, maybe she did know. But this conversation wasn't answering any of her questions. "Where are we going?"

"Far enough that Curtis can't easily reach us, but not so far that it'll be a problem returning once we've dealt with Feud," Riley said.

"He will be looking for hallowed ground," Bane said.

"Somewhere no demon can enter." Riley glanced in the review mirror, grinning.

"You cross me and you will pay," Bane warned.

Aura almost asked Riley if he was crazy. She looked at Bane instead. "Are you planning to hurt us when you're free?"

"You, never. Him, maybe. It will depend on what he does."

Aura held Bane's gaze. "I won't let you hurt him."

Bane grinned. "I wouldn't expect anything less. But I don't have to hurt you to stop you."

His grin was unnerving. As were his words. "Why me?"

"You wouldn't give him the ring until you were certain he would release me. I am not giving you anything in exchange for your concern. Nor am I beholden to you or owe you anything. I choose to offer no harm to you as a courtesy."

She glanced at Riley, not sure what she should say.

"He's making sure there's no claim on him or his power. He plans to grow in strength. Not be permanently kept weak like being bound to Curtis has done to him."

"No one will bind me ever again," Bane vowed. "And Curtis will pay for what he has done to me."

"I can't let you kill him," Riley said. "I will have to stop you. I'm a hunter. We can't allow demons to harm a human no matter what they've done."

"Think you can stop me?" Bane once again smiled.

Chapter Nineteen

Aura looked away from Bane unable to face the unnerving smile any longer. "Are you still setting Bane free?"

Riley nodded. "If he's smart he'll take his freedom and not waste it. If not…" He shrugged, glancing in the mirror again.

Thinking it best to change the topic, Aura asked, "How far are we going?"

"A few hours. You should have a sleep while you can." Riley glanced at her. "It's probably going to be a long night."

She turned in her seat to look at Bane. "How many demons does Curtis have?"

"He had planned to resummon those you sent back, but Feud demanded he help him with the hunter." Bane nodded towards Riley. "He'll call them back tonight and you'll need to face them all again."

"How many does he have now?" Riley asked.

"Only Destruction and Feud." Bane's expression hardened. "And me." There was bitterness and anger in his tone.

Aura automatically rested her hand on Bane's knee, wanting to comfort him. "He won't have you for long." Realising what she'd done, she started to draw her hand away from him.

Bane closed his hand over hers, keeping it in place. "You do realise I am a demon. What kind of hunter are you?"

Riley laughed. "She's obviously one that likes to take risks."

She glared at him. She wasn't the one who kept upsetting Bane. That was him. "I think you're talking about yourself, not me."

Riley glanced at her. "Are you sure, love?"

Her lips parted at his words, but she couldn't think of a reply. She wasn't the one who took risks. She was the sensible one. Like Zinnia. Her mum took all the risks and look how that had worked out for her. She'd ended up living with a serial killer in the making.

Bane let her hand free. "Did you know there are human and demon pairings?"

Aura stared at Bane. "Uhm… what?"

Riley chuckled. "He's asking you out on a date."

Aura's mouth dropped open, her gaze fixed on Bane.

"Demons don't follow that pathetic human ritual. We don't need to figure out what we want. Once we know what we want, we pursue it."

She felt like closing her eyes in the hope this moment wasn't real. The last thing she needed was to be pursued by a demon with some kind of romantic interest in her. Although who knew what a demon considered romantic. "Humans like dating. They like to get to know someone they're interested in. I think most of us are too different as a species for things to work well."

Bane inclined his head. "You're right. I wouldn't be willing to change to suit you."

She barely managed not to stare at him open mouthed again. How had he taken that message from her words? It was past time for another change in topic. "Will Curtis use human sacrifice to summon more demons?"

"He'll wait till three in the morning. That's the best time to summon them," Riley said.

"How are we going to get back there before then?" Aura asked.

"Blake and Allie will take care of things until we can return."

Riley's words didn't reassure her. "What about the people at Blue Sky? What if he uses them to fight Blake and Allie?"

"My blood was used to control them," Bane said.

"Then we need to be close before we set you free. We can't leave my family to deal with that on their own," Riley said.

Aura looked from one to the other. "What does that mean?"

"That Curtis will no longer have any control over them." Bane grinned. "They will be mine."

Aura pointed a finger at him. "They will be set free too. Like you will be."

Bane held her gaze, eventually inclining his head. "Not until I have made Curtis suffer."

"They aren't your army," Riley said. "You will send them away from the fight."

Bane shrugged. "They are all useless. Chosen for their lack of ties rather than their skills. I need no one to help me take down Curtis."

"He will answer to the law," Riley said.

"For summoning demons?" Aura found it difficult to believe he could be locked away for that. Who would believe he'd accomplished that trick?

"No. For human sacrifice," Riley said. "Bane will tell us where to find the proof."

"Now we come to the payment you want," Bane said.

"We can find it without your help. It will be easier with it and assure that Curtis can't escape and will spend his life in prison," Riley said.

"Being looked after for the rest of his life?" Bane demanded. "That is not acceptable."

"It is the only option that is acceptable," Riley stated.

Bane glared at Riley, not replying.

Aura looked from one to the other, wondering if there was a single topic that wouldn't cause an argument. Giving up on having a conversation, she looked out the window, watching the passing scenery.

When they eventually stopped, she blinked, stretching as she realised that at some stage she must have drifted off to sleep. "Where are we?"

"Last stop before our destination." Riley swung the car door open. "I'll put fuel in. If you're hungry there's food in one of the bags in the boot or you can grab some snacks from the servo."

"Okay." She stumbled out of the car, glancing at Bane when he joined her. When he walked beside her, she stopped before entering the building. "You don't need to follow me."

"The world is a dangerous place."

She stared at him. Surely she hadn't gained some sort of demonic bodyguard. "I can take care of myself. Have been doing so for years."

"You will make sure Riley sets me free."

She nearly sighed, barely holding it back. "He'll set you free. You don't need me to make him keep his word."

"I don't trust him."

This time she did sigh. "You're not following me to the restroom." She strode inside, finding him waiting at the door for her when she came out of the restroom. Slowly shaking her head, she chose a packet of chips and headed to the counter.

"That and the fuel?" The attendant nodded to the chips.

Before she could tell him no, Riley entered the building.

"I'm paying." Riley strode up to the counter, holding out a credit card.

She waited until they were in the car before she spoke. "You have a credit card?"

"Yes."

She'd expected more of an answer. "How do you have a credit card? Does hunting demons pay that well?"

Riley laughed. "Not exactly. It's family money. We've been hunting demons for centuries. It's not the kind of job that leaves a lot of time left over for a conventional job."

"Then why are you going to uni?"

Riley started the car, heading back to the road. "Because we're expected to explore other options. Our family wants us to make sure this is what we want with our lives. And, if for any reason anything happens that makes it impossible for us to continue fighting demons, we have something else to fall back on."

"Why do you want to be a psychologist?"

"It's interesting and there aren't a lot of professionals that demon hunters can talk to, about the hazards of the job, without being considered insane."

She smiled. "Sometimes you can be really sweet."

"Only sometimes?"

She glanced at Bane, causing Riley to laugh. She slowly shook her head. "I'm surprised you don't have more demons wanting you dead."

"So am I." Riley pulled up in front of a cemetery, the low iron fence having lost the majority of the white paint years ago. "Want to come for a walk?"

"What for." She eyed him suspiciously.

"To learn the lay of the land."

Her breath caught in her throat. "There's going to be a battle?"

Riley took hold of her hands. "Feud isn't going to allow himself to be easily caught. You can stay in the middle of the cemetery if you want. He won't be able to reach you there."

"I can't help you against Feud unless you order it," Bane said.

"I'm not about to order you to do anything," Riley said. "I believe in free will."

"I cannot help you unless you order it." Bane stressed the last two words.

Aura frowned. "Are you telling us to order you?"

"Now why would I do that?" Bane asked.

"Probably so you can't be held responsible for going against Feud while still having the opportunity to attack him," Riley said.

"Did he hurt you?" Aura asked.

"He never physically harmed me," Bane said.

"Words can hurt too." She could have given him a long list of occasions as proof. Having a strange mum hadn't helped her any during primary school.

"You'll have to order me when he arrives," Bane said. "If you really want me to help."

"Bane-"

The demon interrupted Riley. "Or set me free now."

"I can't risk you interfering with our plans. And we can't let the residents of Blue Sky be caught in something that might get them killed." Riley let go of Aura's hands and got out of the car.

Aura watched Riley walk around to the passenger side of the car, getting out before he reached her door. She glanced at Bane who seemed determined to remain at her side. "What are our plans exactly?"

Riley looked at Bane, remaining silent a moment before he spoke. "We'll bind him to a ring."

"You would keep him bound to you and use him for your own means?" Bane demanded.

Riley shook his head. "He'll be sent to a secure place on hallowed ground. He will be imprisoned, not used against his will."

"There's no guarantee he'll remain imprisoned forever," Bane said.

Riley grinned. "I doubt he'll escape in my lifetime." His grin was replaced by a rare expression of seriousness. "I'd understand if you feel uncomfortable about another demon being bound to a ring."

Aura nearly backed away when Bane's unnerving smile appeared.

"As I said earlier you'll have to order me to help when he arrives."

Riley inclined his head. "We're going to walk around the outside of the cemetery to choose the best location."

Bane waved Riley forward. "Lead the way."

Aura had hoped Bane would stay behind. She wanted to ask Riley if it was typical for hunters to work with demons. She didn't get the chance until after they'd tramped around the cemetery several times, Bane and Riley arguing locations.

She sat under the only shady tree in the cemetery. It was close to the centre of the place, a timber seat badly in need of repair beneath it. Riley had thrown a picnic blanket over the bench seat to protect them from the splinters. "Do hunters often work with demons?"

"More than you would imagine." He opened up the packet of chips that had been left unopened in Aura's lap. "You sure you don't want something more filling to eat?"

"No. Later. And what do you mean by more than I'd imagine?"

Riley grinned. "Technically, we shouldn't work together at all. But life is never simple."

She helped herself to some chips. Thinking over his

words, she glanced towards Bane where he stood at the edge of the cemetery, his gaze firmly on her. Like that wasn't creepy at all. "When are we setting him free?"

Riley slipped off Bane's ring, taking her left hand. "I don't want to be wearing this when I bind Feud to the other ring. I don't want to risk anything going wrong." He slipped it over her thumb, smiling. "Maybe you should ask him to resize it for you." He slid the ring off, putting it on her middle finger. "He will be able to. Just make sure you keep your hand closed when you ask it of him. Who knows what rules Curtis has used to bind him to the ring." He closed her hand into a fist.

"You're serious."

Riley nodded.

"But-" She glanced between Bane and Riley. "He can resize a ring."

"Yes. Tell him you don't want to risk losing it in the fight."

"Well of course I don't want to risk losing it, but…" Her voice trailed off as she tried to once more accept the impossible.

"Don't ask it as a favour. Make sure he understands he's doing it for himself," Riley said. "Never ask a demon for a favour."

"Okay." She rose to her feet, trying to ignore the uncertainty she heard in her voice. That wasn't something she was accustomed to hearing. "I'll ask-" She broke off, taking a deep breath. "I'll make the suggestion."

Riley grinned. "You're a natural."

"I don't know about that." She strode towards Bane, thinking about her limited fighting skills. Riley could use a bow and a sword and who knew what else. She could throw daggers and joust. Not very handy at all. She stopped in front of Bane, making sure she was out of the cemetery first. She held out her hand, keeping it curled into a fist. "Riley wants me to wear the ring so nothing happens to it in the fight against Feud."

Bane inclined his head. "Thank you for telling me."

"I'm not sure that's a good idea. It's loose on me and might fall off."

"Are you making a request?"

She would have to tell Riley she wasn't as much of a natural as he thought. "I wanted you to know in case you wanted to do something about it. Like resizing it. After all, you're the one who'd find it a problem if someone else found it."

Bane grinned. "Give it time and you might end up being as devious as a demon."

"Is that meant to be a compliment?"

Bane placed his hand over hers. "Could it be anything else?"

Chapter Twenty

Aura decided it was probably best not to point out to Bane that some people might take his words as an insult. "What-" She broke off when the ring tightened on her finger, making her question unnecessary. About to thank him, she stopped. Would he take it as having done her a favour? Dealing with demons was a lot more difficult than she'd initially thought. Some holy water, a few weapons and prayers were the easy way. "I'm glad I won't risk losing your ring."

He opened her hand, holding her fingers, his gaze on the ring. "You will set me free once Feud is trapped."

"When we're close to Blue Sky, like Riley said."

Bane inclined his head and let go of her hand.

She stood in front of him, not knowing what to do or say, unnerved by the grin that appeared. Turning, she strode back to Riley, glancing at the ring. It looked exactly the same. The only difference was it fit properly. She sat on the seat beside Riley. "What do we do now?"

"Wait for dark and the arrival of Feud." He rose from the seat. "I'm going to grab the swag out of the boot and have a rest before then. Unless you want a sleep?"

She shook her head, not at all tired after her nap in the car. "Can you sleep in a cemetery?"

Riley laughed. "From the look of this place I doubt anyone comes out here, but if they do they'll probably chase us away."

She watched him go. Why wasn't he more concerned about that? Didn't they need to remain here? She met him halfway back from the car, the swag on his shoulder. "Where will we go if someone kicks us out?"

"For a drive and return at sunset."

"Won't Feud get us?"

Riley rolled the swag out under the tree. "He'll need to travel here from the last place he was at. We'll have a bit of time to get ready before he arrives."

"Oh." She watched him stretch out on the swag, smiling when he saw she watched him. Returning his smile, she sat on the seat again, glancing around the cemetery. It was going to be a very long wait until Feud arrived.

The afternoon passed slower than she expected. She wandered amongst the graves, pausing to read some of the inscriptions, had a nap on the seat and then returned to pacing. A few times she glanced at Bane, each time finding he watched her. She wasn't tempted to talk to him. In some ways it reminded her of how the murderer had occasionally watched her and her mum. And that was certainly something she didn't want to think about right now. Not with night slowly approaching.

When Riley woke late afternoon, he prepared food at the back of the car, setting up a camp table and small gas hotplate. As darkness fell the gear was packed away, except for the picnic blanket, and they sat on the seat with a lantern at their feet.

Aura leaned against Riley's side, his arm around her shoulders, staring up at the stars. "How will we know he's coming?"

He brushed his fingers across her wrist. "We'll know."

"Oh." She'd forgotten about that. "How do you bind a demon to a piece of jewellery?"

Riley grinned "With great difficulty. I have to recite a binding ritual. If the demon was willing it'd be a lot easier, but I've got a feeling he's going to fight it every step of the way."

"How do you know a binding ritual? Is it something you use often?"

"It's something most hunters never have the chance to use, but it's one of the things we learn and hope we never have a reason to use it."

She ran her fingers across part of his demon mark. "How many demons did it take to make it this long?"

Riley shrugged, capturing her hand. "I don't keep count."

"What about your brother? Has he kept count?"

His fingers slid between hers and he turned slightly so he could meet her gaze. "You don't have to help. If you're worried you can remain here and be safe from Feud."

"I'm worried, but I will help." She didn't care what he said about having done the right thing by leaving him behind. She wasn't about to do that again. "Even though I have no idea what to do."

"Fight him. We need to weaken him without sending him back to hell. Then I need to use his blood and my blood to bind him to the ring, holding it between us while I recite the ritual."

She stared at him open mouthed. "You've got to do what?"

Riley chuckled. "I told you it'd be easier if he was agreeable."

She slowly shook her head. "You're insane."

"Possibly." He shrugged. "But it doesn't change what needs to be done."

Before she could beg him to come up with a different plan, she felt an itch in her demon mark, the sensation increasing and becoming more like a burn. "He's coming."

Riley picked up the lantern. "He's almost here." He strode to the location they'd chosen for their battle, setting the lantern out of the way. At his feet were his bow and quiver of arrows, a bottle of holy water and the water blaster beside them. "Offer these to Bane once you've given him orders." He indicated the bow and arrows.

When he started to step away from her, she drew him close, holding him tight as she kissed him. "Be careful."

Riley grinned. "You do realise I'm about to fight a demon."

"Yeah. So be careful."

He kissed her before he pulled away and strode out of the cemetery. He held his sword ready, not moving when Feud arrived, stopping directly in front, towering above him.

"You surprise me hunter. I thought you would be cowering in there." Feud gestured towards the cemetery.

"Last chance, Feud. Forget about coming after me and return to hell," Riley said.

Feud threw back his head, laughing. "You think you can best me?"

"I think I can do far better than that." Riley attacked, jumping back when Feud clapped his hands together and summoned a sword.

Aura gathered up the bow and arrows, running to the edge of the cemetery. "Bane."

He came out of the shadows, stopping directly in front of her. "I am here. What are your orders?"

She wasn't sure if she should trust him with weapons. "Help Riley capture Feud." She held out the bow and arrows.

Bane grinned. "It is a pleasure to hold a weapon again after so many decades of being denied one."

Before she could take them back, worried about why Curtis hadn't trusted him with any weapons, he joined the fight. He fired arrows at Feud who roared each time they struck him. She ran back to the water blaster, grabbing it and the bottle of holy water before racing to the edge of the cemetery closest to the fight.

Feud roared when a stream of holy water hit him,

turning towards Aura. "Come out here and face me, human." An arrow struck him and he turned to Bane with another roar. "You will regret taking up arms against me."

"The girl has the ring. You will have to complain to Curtis for letting her take it from him. I must do as she orders." Bane shot Feud again.

Feud blocked the arrow, spinning to clash swords with Riley. There was a flurry of attacks and Riley was driven back. Feud staggered when Aura threw a dagger at him, quickly followed by the second one. She returned to using the water blaster.

Riley lunged for Feud, striking him at the same time as an arrow, blood streaking Feud's body. Riley leapt back out of the way, brushing his hand lightly along the blade of his sword, cutting the heel of his palm. He dodged the next attack, removing the ring and again lunging for Feud, wrapping his arms around him as he dropped his sword.

"Help hold him, Bane." Aura sprayed Feud one last time, not wanting to risk getting holy water on Bane since he was helping them. Dropping the blaster, she dashed forward and grabbed one of the daggers Feud had pulled from his body and dropped on the ground. But it was impossible to use it. Feud fought against Riley and Bane, determined to escape. Dropping the dagger, she wrapped her arms around Feud's arm that he managed to free from Bane, the other one still trapped.

"I will make you both pay," Feud bellowed.

She clung to his arm, jarred by his efforts to shake her off. She wanted to tell Riley to hurry with his recitation. She doubted she could hold on for much longer. Just when she thought it would be impossible to hold him a moment longer, the air was filled with a sensation of power and she was flung back from Feud who disappeared. Bane and Riley were flung aside too. Her body ached and she wanted to remain where she was, unmoving. She forced herself to her feet, staggering over to Riley who remained still.

He opened his eyes, grinning when he spotted her. "That isn't something I want to experience every day."

Bane joined them, holding out a hand to Riley. "Now we return to Blue Sky so you can set me free."

Riley took Bane's hand, allowing the demon to help him to his feet. "We'll go to Colin and Judy's farm. That will be close enough." He slipped Feud's ring on his finger, looking down at his blood-streaked body. "Good thing I wear black." Grinning, he turned to Aura. "You okay?"

She nodded, not bothering to tell him she felt like

she'd been pummelled and every bit of her ached. He didn't look like he'd fared much better. "You're not getting in the car like that, are you?"

She glanced at Bane, frowning when she saw him pick up a pebble from the ground where she had landed.

"I'll clean up a bit before I get in the car." Riley gathered his weapons and the picnic blanket then collected the lantern and examined the ground.

She collected her daggers and the water blaster, putting them in the car before she checked what Riley was up to. "What are you doing?" Aura moved closer to him, but couldn't see anything out of the ordinary.

"Looking for blood."

She eyed him up and down. "Have you considered looking in a mirror?"

Riley laughed, rising to his feet. "That isn't the blood I'm concerned about. It's leaving any behind for other demons to find." He strode to the car, taking out a cloth and wiping most of the blood off himself. He put the cloth in a plastic bag and tucked it away in one of the bags in the boot before facing Aura. "You ready to go?"

Her attention was caught by Bane who paced the

area, his gaze scanning the ground. She started to ask what he was looking for.

"Aura?" Riley moved closer to her, holding out a second cloth. "Are you ready?"

"Yeah." She took the cloth and wiped Feud's blood off her. "I'm ready." The sooner they set Bane free the sooner they could rescue the rest of the people kept at Blue Sky. Although she had no idea how they were going to deal with people who had probably faced things they hadn't even thought existed. No wonder Riley wanted to be a psychologist. Who else was there for demon victims to talk to? She got in the car. "Are you only planning to see hunters when you finish studying?"

"No." Riley started the car. "Anyone who has encountered demons."

She turned to look at Bane who was sitting in the back. "Are you okay?" He stared back at her, his expression difficult to see clearly in the limited light from the dash. She was about to ask him again, when he spoke.

"Why are you concerned about my well being?"

"Because you helped."

"You ordered me."

She started to disagree.

He interrupted her. "You ordered me. I had to

follow orders." He spoke the words slower and more forcefully.

"Okay. I ordered you, but I can check that you're okay and my orders didn't get you hurt."

Again he didn't answer immediately. "I am unharmed."

She nodded, facing forward again, setting the bloodstained cloth beside her on the seat.

"You should have a sleep while you can," Riley said.

"What's with you always telling me to sleep?" Aura asked.

"Because sometimes we have to sleep while we can. Demons can appear day or night, depending on their power," Riley said.

"Is it only you and your brother and a handful of cousins?"

Riley laughed. "No, but the world is a big place and there are more demons than there are hunters. Luckily most of them remain in hell."

She glanced at him several times, trying to figure out why he wasn't bothered by that. They were outnumbered. "Why don't you recruit more hunters?"

"Because not everyone is suited to the job and it's hard to know who would join the fight and who would fall apart at the thought that demons exist." Riley momentarily rested his hand on her leg. "Not everyone has your strength."

She stared at him. Strength? That was news to her. Her heart had not long slowed after their fight and she dreaded to think of the one to come. Instead of remarking on his comment, she remained silent, the drone of the engine eventually sending her to sleep. She woke disorientated, the night coming back to her in vivid images. The engine was silent. "We're here?" She looked towards Riley who sat beside her, a shadow in the darkness.

"I was about to wake you," Riley said.

"Is anyone else here?" She looked through the windscreen at the house, the verandah light on, the rest of the place dark.

"I don't know. Probably not. Blake and Allie should be keeping an eye on things at Blue Sky to make sure Curtis doesn't do anything drastic." Riley opened the car door.

Aura reached for him, resting her hand on his arm when he remained in the car. "How strong is Destruction? Will we be able to send her back to hell?"

"That will depend on what deal she made with Curtis," Riley said.

"Destruction's son ran afoul of a demon who owed Curtis a favour. In return for claiming that favour on her son's behalf, Destruction has to answer to Curtis for the eighty years the other demon has agreed to postpone his hunt," Bane said.

Chapter Twenty-One

Aura turned in the car so she could face Bane. Not that it helped. There were too many shadows to see him clearly. "That sounds complicated. Why couldn't Destruction strike a deal directly with the demon her son upset?"

"He had no reason to strike a deal with her. He would rather torture her son for an eternity. But since he owed Curtis a favour, he has postponed his revenge," Bane said.

"Then why does she want to slice Curtis into little pieces?" It didn't make sense to Aura. Surely Destruction should be grateful.

"Curtis is good at making enemies. It is only that he's better at doing favours for demons that he's lasted this long. It would have been interesting to see how he managed to avoid Destruction's plans for him. Once the favour expires, she has no reason to keep him alive. When Curtis dies, she'll have no reason to keep anyone alive. The moment the demon learns of Curtis' death, their deal is voided and Destruction's son is in danger again."

"We're not going to kill Curtis." When Bane didn't answer, she said. "Bane? Did you hear me?"

Bane opened the door. "I heard."

"But he's not interested in listening," Riley said.

"What I am interested in is being released." Bane got out of the car.

Aura sighed, half tempted to tell Riley not to set him free yet. But that would be wrong after all Bane had done to help them. She removed the ring, holding it out to Riley. "What do we need to do?"

Riley slipped the ring on his little finger before he got out of the car. "I order you to remain there." He pointed to a spot ten metres from the car.

"Riley-"

He interrupted her protests. "We don't want him leaving before we start the process. He'll want to do everything in his power to stop us. He's already told us that."

"The hunter is correct," Bane said. "The moment he puts oil on the ring I'll be compelled to attack or flee. This way I'm forced to remain on this spot."

Riley took out a scrap of rust stained cloth, giving

it to Aura. "Hold it up so I can tip some holy water on it to dampen the blood."

She nearly dropped the cloth when she learned what was on it. "Why didn't you tell me those marks are blood?"

Riley sprinkled holy water on the cloth. He looked at his hands then tipped some over them, washing off the bloodstains, drying his hands on the seat of his jeans. "Throw a dagger at him. I need his blood too."

"I'm not about-"

Bane interrupted her. "Do you have a dagger that has no holy water on it?"

"The holy water will help break the binding quicker." Riley took out the vial of oil, opening it to tip a few drops on his thumb. He made the sign of the cross on the ring with the oil. "Be sealed with the gift of the Holy Spirit."

Bane hissed as the oil seemed to sink into the ring.

"What's happening?" Aura took a step towards the demon.

"Blood, now," Riley ordered. He took the cloth from her and smeared it across the ring before striding towards Bane, letting the cloth fall to the ground. He glanced over his shoulder. "Throw the dagger." He stopped in front of Bane, out of arm's reach. "Hold out your hand, away from your body so Aura can target it."

She held the dagger tightly, her gaze on Bane's hand. The thin grey fingers were stretched out and she took a deep breath, trying not to think about what she was about to do.

"Don't make him wait. That's crueller than getting it over and done with," Riley said.

She threw the dagger, wincing when Bane howled, ripping the dagger from his hand to throw it on the ground. At the same time, she felt an itch in her demon mark. Was that from attacking Bane?

Riley looked past Bane. "We need to get this done in a hurry. Demon coming in fast." He grabbed hold of Bane's hand.

The demon tried to escape, his feet remaining where they were planted, his other hand trying to push Riley away.

Aura glanced between Bane and the direction of Blue Sky. A demon was coming? The only demon left, as far as she knew, was Destruction. This couldn't be good. When Bane knocked Riley to the ground, the hunter continuing to cling to the demon's hand, she ran forward, trying to capture Bane's free arm.

Riley struggled to his feet. "No longer bound to

this ring we hold between us. No longer in service to those who have possession of it."

"Move away, Aura. You will be hurt," Bane said.

She clung to his arm while Riley repeated the words. "I can't." She gritted her teeth together, desperately clinging to him as he tried to fling her off. How long would this take? But she couldn't ask. She needed all her energy to hold on.

Bane roared, throwing his head back as he went to his knees.

The action partially broke Aura's grip and she was flung from him to lie sprawled on the ground, the wind knocked from her. Before she could rise, the stars were blocked by Destruction, a sword raised above her. Aura tried to scramble backwards, expecting the blade to slice into her. The moment stretched out as the blade came towards her.

Destruction howled, staggering forward, the blade missing Aura. Destruction faced the other direction, an arrow protruding from her back, dark blood staining her dress.

Aura stumbled to her feet, grabbing her last dagger, trying to process the fact she was alive. She saw Allie standing on the other side of Destruction. A glance around showed the hunter was alone.

Allie drew back another arrow. "Come on, bitch. Make my day." She fired the arrow.

Destruction took a step towards Allie, spinning to face Aura when she threw her dagger. The demon growled and leapt for Aura who reached for a vial of holy water, the only weapon she had left.

Bane leapt on Destruction, driving her to the ground. "My human."

"You can find another plaything. Curtis wants this one dead." Destruction fought to escape, clawing at Bane.

Roaring, blood dripping down his face, Bane escaped her grip, backing away. "I'm no longer bound to him." He held up his hand, the ring now on one of his long, narrow fingers. "He will pay for all he's done." With one of his unnerving grins, he ran in the direction of Blue Sky.

"I will destroy you." Destruction raced after him.

"That can't be good." Allie lowered her bow.

Riley glanced around the area. "Where's Blake?"

"Keeping an eye on things. Curtis is getting ready for his three a.m. sacrifice," Allie said.

Riley strode towards the motorbike. "I'll meet the two of you over there."

Aura ran after him, grabbing hold of his arm. "Not on your own."

He pulled out of her grip and started the motorbike. "I can't take two passengers."

"Both of you go. I'll catch up. Blake is over there alone." Allie ran towards Blue Sky, not waiting for a reply.

"Get on and hold tight," Riley warned.

"My daggers-" Aura gestured towards the ground where they'd landed.

"No time. There's a dagger in my boot you can have." He took off the moment she was seated behind him.

Aura clung to Riley, pressing close to him as they raced through the night, jumping potholes and taking the corners too fast for her liking. Closing her eyes didn't help and she was tempted to tell him it wouldn't help if he ended up killing them before they could arrive.

Riley pulled up in a spray of dirt, cutting the engine. "Move. It feels like he's starting the ritual early."

Aura got off the motorbike, rubbing her demon mark. She took the dagger Riley handed her, following him when he broke into a run. "Where are we going?"

"To the pentagram." Riley headed for the back of the house.

Aura followed Riley around the corner to find Bane and Destruction fighting. Destruction broke free from Bane and smashed a window, jumping inside the house. Aura reached Bane before he could follow her. She grabbed hold of his arm. "The residents. You have to send them to safety." She waved Riley on when he slowed and looked over his shoulder. Someone needed to help Blake stop Curtis.

Bane shook her hand from his arm. "De will help him escape."

"Let the hunters take care of him for now. How long will it take to send the residents to safety?" Again she grabbed hold of his arm. "Please, Bane. Don't let them be killed."

Bane grinned.

She nearly let go of his arm and stepped back. Instead she tightened her grip and tried to think of a reason it'd help him. "Curtis can hide behind them. Send them to safety and there will be less between you and Curtis. Send them to Judy's kitchen. Tell them to wait there until a demon hunter comes for them."

"What will you offer me in exchange for saving them?" Bane asked. "For saving all of them."

She fought the urge to close her eyes, continuing to look into Bane's, the flicker of flames noticeable in the shadows. She wanted to tell him she didn't make deals with demons, Riley's warning ringing in her head. "What do you want?"

"What will you offer?"

She tried to ignore the pound of her heart and the shiver that ran down her spine. "Anything." The word came out as little more than a whisper.

"Most humans aren't willing to sacrifice themselves for others." He pulled out of her grip, his smile not dimming. "No deal."

She started to protest.

"I was interested to know how far you were willing to go. You surprised me. I'll send them to Judy's kitchen. They'll remain there until you tell them your name. Only you." He pointed a finger at her. "You better make sure you survive or they'll remain in Judy's kitchen until they die. Unable to go anywhere else." He dashed through the window.

Aura stared after him, mouth hanging open. It took her a few seconds to move. Relief and fear rushed through her. He was making the lives of those people hinge on her surviving? She wanted to run after him and tell him to take it back. To make it so any of the hunters could release them from the orders he was going to give them.

Before she could enter the window, a woman

climbed out, a vacant expression visible on her face for the few seconds it was lit from the bedroom light. The woman strode towards Colin and Judy's farm. She stared after the woman for a moment before heading inside, searching for the hunters. After a minute she realised all she had to do was follow her demon mark. The closer she came to Destruction, the more it bothered her mark. Hearing the clash of swords, she broke into a run. They were in a different room to the pentagram. The three demon hunters, Curtis and Destruction. She had no idea where Bane was. Hopefully he was rescuing all the residents.

Riley attacked Curtis while the other two attacked Destruction, the three of them wielding swords. Aura remained near the doorway, clutching the dagger, having no idea how she could help. She smiled, beginning to pray.

Bane rushed into the room, pushing her against the wall, his hand clamping over her mouth, taking the dagger from her with the other. "Don't." He shook his head. "No praying."

Fear burst through her until she met his gaze. There was pain in his eyes, but no anger. Unable to protest with how tight his hand pressed against her mouth, she tried to shake her head. It was impossible.

He loosened his grip. "Understand?" He lowered his hand, grasping her shoulder to keep her in place.

"Sorry." She glanced past him. "Only Destruction was in here when I started."

He tilted his head slightly, examining her. A smile formed. "You mean your words." He laughed, letting her go and spinning to face the room.

Before she could ask what amused him, he was throwing himself at Curtis. The force of his action pushed Curtis out of Riley's reach, knocking the man from his feet. Bane raised the dagger, holding it above Curtis.

Aura took a step towards them. "No!"

Bane plunged the dagger into Curtis, grinning as he raised the dagger and repeated his action.

Aura's legs nearly gave way. "Bane." She took several more steps towards the demon who'd leapt to his feet, dagger still in his hand, to face Riley.

Destruction howled, trying to get to Bane. Allie and Blake continued their attacks so it was impossible for her to do anything other than defend herself. "I will destroy you." Again she tried to get past the hunters. "Do you hear me, Bane? Destroy you."

Riley held his sword ready, continuing to face Bane. "I warned you not to harm any humans. I can't let you get away with killing Curtis."

Bane continued to grin. "You have to catch me first." He darted past Riley, taking Aura's hand to place the dagger in it. "It will be interesting to see where life takes you." He glanced over his shoulder at Destruction who continued to yell threats at him. "Have the hunters bind your son to an object and put it away with Feud. No demon will be able to get him then. Being trapped is probably a better option than an eternity of torture."

Riley strode towards Bane. "You can't remain in this world."

"Can't I?" He grinned at Riley his expression turning fierce when he looked towards Destruction. "Kill my human and I will become involved." He ran a finger down Aura's cheek before running from the room.

Destruction howled, dropping to her knees, her hands splayed against the floor, head thrown back as she made the sound again.

Chapter Twenty-Two

Aura looked from Riley to Destruction, wanting to tell the demon to stop. The noise was sending a shiver down her spine. From the way Allie winced she guessed the hunter felt the same way. Aura raised a hand to wipe Curtis' blood from her cheek.

Riley captured her hand before she could. "Don't. We'll clean it off with holy water. Who knows what Bane did." Riley grinned. "Other than tell you that he plans to be your stalker. For life."

"He what?" Shock struck Aura and again her legs felt weak. Her gaze was drawn to Destruction, the hunters standing in front of her with lowered swords. "Can't you do something to make her stop?"

"I vote we send her back to hell," Allie said. "A gag wouldn't be enough to cope with that noise."

Aura was tempted to agree with Allie. "What about her son? Our actions put him in danger."

"Not our actions," Riley said. "Bane's actions."

"We set Bane free," Aura protested.

"We all have free will." Blake sheathed his sword, looking to Destruction. "And if you don't stop making that noise I will send you back to hell."

"What about her son?" Aura looked at each of them. How did they know Destruction's son was bad?

"He can't protect himself like other demons. Nor could he last an eternity of torture." Destruction glared at them. "He's part human."

Aura stared open mouthed at Destruction, wanting to ask the demon to repeat herself.

Blake slowly shook his head. "I'm not sure a binding would work. Or that it would be ethical since he's part human."

Destruction rose to her feet, tilting her head back to look disdainfully at him. "You would expect me to trust a hunter with the protection of my son?"

"What I don't get is how you ended up having a kid to a human when you don't think much of us," Allie said.

Aura finally closed her mouth. That had been one of her thoughts too.

Destruction looked directly at Aura. "Every once in

a while a human comes along that stands out from the rest."

Aura wanted to protest, but wasn't sure what she was protesting against.

Riley sheathed his sword and took the dagger from Aura. "Are we sending her back to hell?" He looked to his brother.

Blake shook his head. "Not for now." He turned to Destruction. "Warn your son. Get him to safety. You harm a human and we will hunt you down regardless of how vulnerable that makes your son."

Destruction looked at each of them. "Why should I trust anything you say?" She backed away, edging towards a window in the far wall.

Allie shrugged. "That's not our problem."

"Allie Cat," Blake said softly.

"Did you forget she tried to kill us?" Allie sheathed her sword. "I hope you're not expecting me to be her new best friend."

Aura laughed at Allie's comment, the laughter ending when Destruction smashed the window and leapt outside. "Should we be concerned about what she plans to do?" She nodded towards the window.

"Only time will tell," Blake said. "We don't know if her actions were her own or forced upon her by Curtis."

Aura glanced at Curtis, not wanting to look at him too closely. "What are we going to do about him?"

"Clean off the murder weapon for starters," Riley said.

Again Aura found herself standing with her mouth open and words failing her. "I held the murder weapon."

Riley grinned. "So did I."

"Are you insane?" she demanded, her gaze narrowing as she looked at Blake when he laughed. "How could you have let him do that?"

Blake slung an arm around Allie's shoulders. "Clean up crew should be here in about half an hour. I rang them earlier."

"Clean up crew?" Aura turned to Riley who only nodded in answer. "What is a clean up crew?"

"Exactly what it sounds like. Most of the world isn't ready to learn about demons." Riley glanced around the room, his gaze eventually drawn to the doorway. "We should find the inhabitants."

"They're in Judy's kitchen," Aura said.

Riley's expression instantly became serious and he moved closer, his hand taking hers. "What did you do? What did you promise him?"

"Everything and nothing."

Riley momentarily closed his eyes. "He wanted nothing in exchange for his help?"

"No. Only wanted to see how far I was willing to go to save all of them."

Riley slowly shook his head. "In future you'll find another option."

She smiled. "In future."

Riley grinned. "Yeah. In future." He momentarily tightened his grip on her hand. "We should see if they're okay. Want a lift on the bike?"

She pressed her forefinger against his chest. "You better not ride it the same way you did on the way over here. There's no emergency this time."

Blake chuckled, heading for the door, arm in arm with Allie. "Don't hold your breath that it'll be any better." He paused at the doorway. "We'll make sure Bane didn't miss anyone."

Riley inclined his head before returning his attention to Aura. "The ride was exhilarating."

She slowly shook her head, walking beside him. "Not the word I would have used. Death defying is a more accurate description."

Riley laughed. "I'm not the one with a demon stalker. I think you were a little too nice to him."

"What did you expect me to do? Be mean?"

Riley let go of her hand to slip his arm around her

waist. "No. I expected you to do exactly what you did. You wouldn't be you otherwise."

His words caused her lips to curve into a smile. It didn't last long. Worry crowded in. "Is that common? Having a demon stalker."

Riley let go of her to open the front door, the bloody dagger in his other hand. "Demons aren't above using humans for their own ends. So be wary of him."

She nodded. Bane might think he could use her, but she wasn't about to let that happen. Their dealings would be on her terms or not at all. Preferably not at all.

"Some demons also think we're entertainment, others that we're the bottom of the food chain." Riley shrugged. "Who knows how the rest think."

Aura wasn't sure she wanted to know how a demon thought. She stepped through the door, surprised to find a hint of light in the sky. Morning wasn't far off? How had that much time passed?

Riley strode towards the motorbike, looking over his shoulder when she didn't follow. "You okay?"

Blood was smeared across her cheek, she'd been given a murder weapon to hold and there was a demon that planned to check up on her in the future. A smile slowly formed. "I have no idea what I am, but whatever it is, it isn't boring and I don't think there's much balance to it."

Riley laughed, getting on the motorbike and nodding to the seat behind him. "Hop on." He held out the dagger. "You're going to have to hold this again."

She took the dagger before getting on behind him. "Then you better take this trip a little easier than the last one. I wouldn't want to accidentally stab you."

The trip back to Colin and Judy's place was uneventful and the eight people in the kitchen remained motionless until Aura had introduced herself. They also remained calm until they were given holy water to drink. Several panicked and one dropped onto a seat and began to cry. Another made a run for the back door, Riley tackling him and having to talk him into sticking around long enough to find out what was going on.

Aura was relieved when the clean up crew arrived and she could have a shower. Finished in the bathroom, and dressed in a clean pair of jeans and a t-shirt, she searched for Riley. She found him out the front, tinkering with the motorbike.

Riley wiped his hands on a rag, smiling at her as she walked towards him. "Feel better?"

"Apart from feeling tired." And having a few aches

that would probably take a bit to go. She went into his arms when he tossed the rag onto the seat of the motorbike. "Is life always like this for you?"

"Sometimes."

She met his gaze, seeing the wariness past the humour. "Just wanted to know what I was getting myself into."

He chuckled. "Not a great deal of balance I'm afraid."

"I want to learn how to use a sword."

Riley nodded to the verandah. "Your throwing daggers are over there."

"Mine?" She worried at the word like it was a loose tooth, smiling when she decided she like the sound of it. "Mine." She slid her arms around his neck, drawing his head down so she could kiss him.

The sound of a phone ringing drew them apart and Riley smiled down at her. "I better answer that."

She watched him go, her gaze taking in the place once he was out of sight. It hit her. They'd saved Colin and Judy's farm. Saved their home and their lives. Emotions exploded through her and she grinned. No wonder Riley and his family did this. How many people could say they kept the world safe from demons? That they put their lives in danger to do something that mattered. She thought of a few professions, but they didn't interest her. This did. She was still grinning when Riley came out onto the verandah.

"Colin wanted to know when they can come home." Riley came down the stairs. "I told him they could return whenever they want." He wrapped his arms around her. "You ready to go home?"

"Almost."

"What do you need to do before we leave?"

"Get your phone number." Her mum knew where his gran lived and she didn't even have his number.

"Done." He kissed her once more before putting his number in her phone and getting her to add her number to his.

Once they'd said goodbye to the other hunters, and put the rest of their gear in the car, they started the long drive back to Brisbane, Aura drifting off to sleep not long into the drive. They arrived in Brisbane late afternoon and Aura directed Riley to where she lived with her mum, a fibro house that would have been easier to demolish than repair. She sat in the vehicle, not wanting to say goodbye.

Riley opened the car door and got out, looking back in at her for a moment. He closed the door and came around to her side.

She opened the door before he reached her, slowly

getting out of the car. She wanted to tell him to stay, but he'd been away from home longer than she had. Surely there were things he needed to do.

He drew her close. "Is something wrong?"

She started to shake her head, then nodded instead. Demanding when she was going to see him felt awkward. She grinned. "When are you going to teach me how to use a sword?"

Riley chuckled, drawing away from her and capturing her hand. He led her to the boot and took out his sword. "Tonight. I'll bring one for you. In the meantime you might want to get an idea of what one is like to handle."

She took the sword. "Really? Tonight?" She'd worried it'd be days before she saw him again.

"Tonight." He leaned close, lightly kissing her. "Sunset?"

"Yeah." She couldn't stop grinning. "Sunset." She stood on the footpath, holding his sword and her overnight bag until he was out of sight, slowly turning and facing the house. It looked deserted. But that didn't mean anything. Taking a deep breath, she strode towards the house and went around to the back. The door was unlocked and she stepped inside to find her mum and aunt sitting at the kitchen table.

Zinnia looked up from her tablet, a job ad displayed on the screen. "A sword?"

Aura shrugged, not wanting to explain anything right now.

"Everything work out?" Zinnia asked.

Aura nodded. She'd tell Zinnia all the details later. Well, some of them. When her mum wasn't about and not likely to end up thinking demons were something she should get in contact with.

Hazel, who had her back to the door, turned in her seat, holding up a playing card. "Tomorrow will be a good day."

Aura groaned when she saw the ten of hearts her mum held. "Now what?"

"I already told you," Hazel said. "It symbolises a good day. Or at least it stands for good luck and success so since I was asking about tomorrow, it means a good day." She smiled. "I'll do a reading for your day."

Aura turned towards Zinnia who gave her a familiar look. She opened her mouth to tell Zinnia that she was wrong. People could change. She closed it instead, sighing. Not everyone could change or were interested in changing. "I'm going out later."

Hazel finished laying the cards, she'd shuffled, out on the table. "With the sword?"

"Why would she be going out with a sword?" Zinnia demanded.

Hazel held up an eight of diamonds. "The cards say she's getting a new job."

"That's it." Zinnia rose from her seat, starting to gather the cards. "You're not going to keep doing this."

Hazel tried to keep Zinnia from collecting all the cards. "But I haven't finished finding out all the details. What if there's a warning in them for Aura?"

In an effort to distract them, Aura said, "I'm going to become a demon hunter."

Hazel stopped trying to keep Zinnia from the cards. "That's nice." She smiled serenely. "Did you ever find out if you truly can't get wishes out of them?"

"You can't." Aura said the words firmly

"Are you seriously thinking of seeking out demons after everything I've told you? After all you've experienced," Zinnia demanded. "Maybe you're like your father." Zinnia turned to Hazel. "She certainly isn't anything like you." Zinnia faced Aura again. "And nothing like me. There is no way I'd have any further dealings with demons. Even to hunt them down. Do you realise how dangerous that must be?"

Aura looked from one to the other. "You're wrong,

Aunt Zin. I'm like both of you. Somewhere in between. A balance." She grinned. She'd have to tell Riley she'd found that balance he'd suggested would suit her.

"I'll do a reading for your new job the cards told me about." Hazel took the card Zinnia held, adding it to the pile she clutched.

"Hazel!" Zinnia tried to take the playing cards from her sister.

Slowly shaking her head, Aura made her way to her room, deciding to leave them to sort the problem out themselves. She dumped her bag to the side of the door where her other bag had been left. More than likely it had been Zinnia who had put it there. She pushed the items on her duchess towards the mirror that was attached to the back of the duchess, smiling. She placed the sword on the surface. It made her think of the duchess in the room Riley had stayed in. Was his room where he lived filled with weapons? Catching movement in the mirror she spun to face her window.

Her smile faded when she saw Bane sitting on her window ledge. He wasn't as thin and his skin no longer so grey. She started to ask how he'd filled out so quickly, deciding there was another question she needed answered more. "How did you find me?"

He drew a pebble from a pocket, his unsettling smile briefly appearing before he returned the pebble to his pocket. "Your blood. The same way any demon tracks a human."

She stared at the pebble he'd picked up after they'd bound Feud, wanting to demand he return it. She doubted he'd listen. "What are you doing here?"

"There's a demon targeting humans."

"Why are you telling me?"

"Aren't you a hunter?" He nodded to the sword lying across her duchess.

She doubted that was the reason, but she probably had no chance of getting the actual reason out of him if he didn't want to share it. "You do know a blessed house would keep you from coming and going in my room."

Bane rose to his feet, his unnerving smile forming again, remaining in place a lot longer. "You won't do that."

"Why not?"

"Because I'd take it as an insult." He strode towards her, capturing her hand and placing a folded piece of plain paper in it. "The location he was at before sunrise this morning." He walked past her and through the house, his footsteps leading towards the front of the house.

She stared at the empty doorway. How had he managed to return to Brisbane quickly enough to spot a demon harming a human? She'd ask Riley. He should know.

She closed her door. Next time she saw Bane she'd set some rules. Including telling him to stay away from her mum. Her gaze was drawn to the paper and she opened it, seeing an address written in a cursive handwriting, bolder than the one Judy used. For now she'd call Riley and see what he made of this latest development. A grin formed and she thought of the throwing daggers and holy water in her bag. Sword training might have to wait. They had a demon sighting to investigate. She wasn't about to trust Bane. As Riley had pointed out, demons weren't above using humans for their own purposes. She wasn't about to let that happen.

Her hand closed over the handle of the sword. She was a hunter and it was now her job to protect people from demons. And she'd start with making sure this demon wasn't causing trouble.

Chapter Twenty-Three

She stayed close to Riley, her gaze on the shadowy figure of the demon they trailed through the mostly dark streets. They'd been following him since he'd appeared once night had fallen, in the location Bane had given them. If it wasn't for her demon mark she would have thought the demon was human. His muscular body was clothed in regular clothes and his features were ordinary. She glanced at the sword Riley had in a scabbard on his back, not sure wandering the streets of Brisbane with weapons was a good idea. Not that she knew what would be a good idea since they were following a demon.

"Is he going to do anything?" She wasn't sure she liked waiting around to see what the demon was up to. It was much easier when you could immediately attack and send them straight to hell.

"We'll give him a couple of hours."

"Hasn't it been that already?"

Riley laughed softly. "Barely an hour."

She breathed out heavily. "This isn't what-" She broke off when the demon darted down a side street. "We're losing him."

Riley lightly touched her wrist. "No we're not."

"Oh. Of course." It was going to take time getting used to being able to sense when demons were in an area. Who was she kidding? It was going to take time getting used to the notion that demons actually existed.

A shout had both of them breaking into a run and they came around the corner to find the demon had a man on the ground, a dagger raised.

"Let him go." Riley drew his sword as he kept running.

The demon glanced at them, laughing. The dagger plunged towards the man.

Aura came to a stop, throwing one of her daggers at the demon, aiming for his shoulder. She grinned when she hit her target.

The demon howled, the man managing to escape the injured demon, grabbing the dagger he'd dropped. The man stumbled to his feet, holding the dagger out as he slowly backed away from the demon. "Stay back." The man kept the dagger pointed at the demon who drew the throwing dagger from his shoulder.

"Drop the weapon and run," Riley ordered the man.

He looked at each of them. "What is going on? Who are you?"

Aura strode towards the demon, her second throwing dagger in her hand. "You really don't want to know. Be glad you're alive."

The man kept backing away, the demon keeping pace with him.

"Now," Riley ordered.

Aura sighed when the man continued to slowly back away. "Doesn't anyone have a sense of self preservation these days?"

"I'm not about to turn my back on any of you," the man said.

"That won't help you." The demon leapt for the man, moving extremely fast.

Riley tossed holy water on the demon, getting between him and the man, blocking his attack with the sword. The man turned and ran as Riley fought the demon. "Don't let him get away with the demonic weapon."

Aura's gaze narrowed. There was no way she could catch him. A streetlight glinted off the dagger the man carried as he began to turn a corner. Taking a deep breath, she threw her dagger, grinning when she knocked the weapon from his hand. He slowed, looking down at the dagger then over his shoulder, picking up his pace when Aura ran towards him.

"Don't hurt him." Riley fought the demon who used the throwing dagger he'd pulled from his shoulder.

"Hadn't planned to." Reaching the weapons, Aura scooped them up. She glanced at her demon mark, noticing an increase in the sensation. There was another demon in the area? A scan of her surroundings didn't help. Mentally shrugging, she returned to where Riley fought the demon, annoyed the creature was using one of her weapons against Riley. She threw her second dagger at the demon before attacking him with his own weapon.

Riley began to pray, causing the demon to curse him. He grinned. "Your curses are wasted on me. Return to hell and make this easier on yourself." He returned to praying.

Aura joined Riley in praying, darting in and striking the demon with the dagger. When he hissed, she wanted to tell him that would teach him for thinking he could use a hunter's weapon against another hunter. But she wasn't about to stop her praying. Again she slashed him with his dagger, blood staining his clothes. Before she could attack again he vanished, becoming mist that rapidly dispersed. The sensation of an approaching demon increased and she spun to face the direction, lowering the dagger when she saw it was Bane.

Riley kept his sword up. "I didn't think you'd be stupid enough to face me after killing Curtis."

Bane gestured in the direction the man had run. "One human life for another."

Riley didn't lower his sword. "It doesn't work like that. Humans aren't interchangeable."

"How many will it take for you to accept Curtis was mine to kill?"

Riley finally lowered his sword. "You can't atone for a murder that way."

Aura gathered her weapons, sheathing them before she stood at Riley's side, continuing to hold the demon's dagger, her hands at her sides. "How do we know you're not going to go after other humans?"

"I give you my word I have no plans to go after anyone other than those who'll increase my power or who come after me." Bane looked at Riley again. "You plan to train her." He nodded his head in Aura's direction.

"Not because you want me to," Riley said.

Bane's unnerving smile appeared. "For now our goals coincide. Keep her safe and I'll have no need to come after you." He shrugged. "I dare say I'll grow bored of her and this city and eventually move on. But for now I'm intrigued and I plan to stay. I'm not about to let you stop me. So how many lives will it take to make you accept that Curtis' death was inevitable?"

Aura looked between Bane and Riley. "I don't want this to end badly." For some reason she felt responsible for Bane. It was illogical. Probably not at all suitable for a hunter. Her gaze returned to Riley. "He was a slave to Curtis all those years."

Riley sheathed his sword. "That doesn't make what he did right."

"Even amongst us humans there's such a thing as extenuating circumstances," Aura said.

Riley held her gaze a moment before he looked at Bane. "I won't make a deal with a demon. It's simple. You don't harm humans. You don't stand by and let other demons harm humans. That's as bad as harming them yourself."

"What about demons that don't harm humans? Will you get rid of them for me?" Bane asked.

"We're not your personal hunters," Riley stated.

Bane's unnerving smile reappeared. "But you will hunt down those I find who've harmed a human."

"We never return a demon to hell without proof," Riley said.

Bane continued to smile.

Aura wanted to tell him to stop. She'd rather him frown or something. Anything other than his smile that sent a chill down her spine. "Don't push it, Bane."

Bane took a step towards Aura. "I will gain the power I once should have had. It isn't humans I'll gain it from. It's demons." He took the demonic dagger from her. "You will be kept busy."

He was gone before she could protest. She stared along the street. "What just happened?"

"Probably nothing good." Riley glanced around the street. "Time to go in case that man called the cops."

She walked at his side, linking her fingers through his. "How bad is it?"

Riley chuckled. "And they complain I do stupid things. You make me look sensible in comparison."

"That bad?"

"Or that good. Depending on your perspective." He tightened his grip on her hand. "He's a demon. If he gets out of control we'll call on other hunters to help return him to hell. For now, I'll let you claim extenuating circumstances on his behalf."

She started to protest that wasn't what she'd been trying to do, but stopped, not sure what she'd been trying to accomplish with her comment. "How can it be good?"

Riley grinned. "If you're interested in having an endless supply of demons to return to hell then this is good."

"Good?" She worried at the word trying to decide how she felt. Before she could come to a decision Bane was in front of her, holding out a folded piece of paper.

"Take it," Bane ordered.

"What is it?"

"A pathetically weak demon who is stalking an equally pathetic and weak human."

She eyed the paper, trying to make sense of the explanation. "What?"

Bane grabbed her hand and slapped the paper against her palm. "I wouldn't take too long if I were you. I'm not going to keep the human safe all night." He strode away.

Aura looked from the disappearing figure of Bane to the paper she held, letting go of Riley's hand to open it. "An address?"

Riley took the paper from her, tilting it so the streetlight fell across it. "What do you say?" He met her gaze, grinning. "How about doing something stupid?"

A grin slowly formed. "I think your family are wrong."

"Do you? About what?"

"If this is you doing something stupid, then I'm all for it." She brushed her fingers across her sheathed dagger. Maybe having Bane in her life wouldn't be too bad. "Looks like we have a pathetic human to rescue."

Riley chuckled, capturing her hand as they strode back to his car. "I like the way you think." He chuckled again. "Actually, I like more than the way you think."

She grinned, startled by the thought that struck her. Something good had come from one of her mum's disasters. Although it had started as Zinnia's trouble first. It was probably more dangerous than a potential serial killer, but for once that didn't bother her. Reaching the vehicle, she turned to face him, letting go of his hand and sliding her hands over his chest to link them behind his neck. "Who needs a nice safe life when there are demons to hunt?" Her lips met his as his arms went around her. When she pulled back, she met his gaze, enough light from the nearby streetlight to see his warm, brown eyes. "I like the way you think too. Now we better save that human before Bane rethinks keeping them safe." She grinned. "I've got a feeling he isn't all that patient." Not that she could blame him after how many years he'd spent as a slave to Curtis.

Getting in the car, she smiled as Riley put the address in the GPS. How many demons could they hunt in one night? Her smile widened into a grin. It looked like she might have the chance to find out.

Free Ebook

Subscribe to Avril's newsletter and receive a free ebook. This ebook is exclusive to those on her mailing list. To find out more about this offer visit:

www.avrilsabine.com/free-ebook

*

We value your privacy and will not sell, rent, exchange or loan your email address to third parties. Your information is confidential and you are under no obligation to remain on the mailing list and can unsubscribe at any time.

Acknowledgements

As always thanks to my usual crew. Your help is always appreciated.

To The Reader

If you enjoyed this book, why not consider leaving a review to help other readers discover it too? Reader engagement is one of the few ways that lets an author know readers want more books in a particular series or genre. So leave a review and tell friends, not only about this book but also about other ones you've enjoyed, so you can continue to enjoy books by your favourite authors for years to come.

Dreams are meant to be lived,

Avril.

About The Author

Avril is an Australian author who lives with her family on acreage in South East Queensland. She writes mostly young adult and children's speculative fiction, but has been known to dabble in other genres. You can find more information about her at www.avrilsabine.com where you can also subscribe to her newsletter to be kept informed about new releases, current projects, blog posts and exclusive news.

Titles By Avril Sabine

Stories about strong characters and characters who discover their strengths.

SERIES

Assassins Of The Dead- Young Adult Fantasy/ Paranormal

Book 1: Dark Blade

Book 2: Dragon Touched

Book 3: Society Against Vampires

Book 4: King's Request

Dragon Blood- Young Adult Urban Fantasy (with elements of romance)

(5 book series)

Book 1: Pliethin

Book 2: Wyvern

Book 3: Surety

Book 4: Knight

Book 5: Mage

Dragon Mage- Young Adult Urban Fantasy (with elements of romance)

(Series two of Dragon Blood series)

Book 1: Promise

Dragon Blood Chronicles- Young Adult Urban Fantasy (with elements of romance)

(Companion stand alone series to Dragon Blood)

Book 1: Oath

Book 2: Betrayed

Guardians Of The Round Table- Young Adult Fantasy LitRPG

(Co-written with Storm and Rhys Petersen)

Book 1: Dexterity Fail

Book 2: Goblin Boots

Book 3: Singed Feathers

Book 4: Frog Mage

Book 5: Crystal Mine

Book 6: Cursed Harp

Rosie's Rangers- Young Adult Western Steampunk

(6 book series)

Book 1: Justice

Book 2: Vengeance

Book 3: Treachery

Book 4: Accused

Book 5: Wanted

Book 6: Corruption

Mark Of Kings- Children's Fantasy

(Upper middle grade/preteen)

(4 book series)

Book 1: The Arena

Book 2: The Island

Book 3: The Assassin

Book 4: The King

STAND ALONE SERIES

*Demon Hunters- Young Adult Urban Fantasy/
Horror (with elements of romance)*

Book 1: Blood Sacrifice

Book 2: Retribution

Book 3: Tainted

Book 4: Premonition

Book 5: Cursed

Book 6: Feud

Book 7: Extrication

Plea Of The Damned- Young Adult Urban Fantasy/Paranormal

(6 book series)

Book 1: Forgive Me Lucy

Book 2: Forgive Me Aiden

Book 3: Forgive Me Jena

Book 4: Forgive Me Kobe
Book 5: Forgive Me Marti

Book 6: Forgive Me Dawson

Realms Of The Fae- Young Adult Urban Fantasy
(with elements of romance)

The Sword (short story in Like A Girl Anthology)

Heart Of Stone

Book 1: A Debt Owed

Book 2: Marked By The Hunt

Book 3: The Magic Collector

Book 4: An Unexpected Betrayal

Book 5: Imprisoned By Iron

Fairytales Retold (Short Stories)

Snow-White And Rose-Red

The Twelve Brothers

The Light Princess

Beauty And The Beast

Sleeping Beauty

Aschenputtel

The Golden Bird

The Frog Prince

The Death Of Koshchei The Deathless

Myths And Legends Retold (Short Stories)

Ion, Son Of Apollo

Sir Gawain And The Maid With The Narrow Sleeves

Princess Ilse, The Giant's Daughter

YOUNG ADULT NOVELS

Young Adult Fantasy (with elements of romance)

Elf Sight

Earth Bound

Young Adult Urban Fantasy

Stone Warrior (with elements of romance)

The Jungle Inside

Young Adult Contemporary (with elements of romance)

Through Your Eyes

The Ugly Stepsister

Perfect Little Princess

Young Adult Contemporary/Paranormal

Whispers In The Dark (with elements of romance and same sex relationships)

Over Too Soon (with elements of romance)

Young Adult Sci-Fi

Experiment X-One-Six (Urban Sci-Fi/Superheroes)

An Endless Dawn (Post Apocalyptic Sci-Fi)

CHILDREN'S BOOKS

Dragon Lord (Preteen/early teens) (Fantasy)

The Irish Wizard (Upper middle grade) (Urban Fantasy)

SHORT STORIES

Urban Fantasy

Eternally Late

Dealings With Joe

Glimpses (short story in That Moment When Anthology)

Contemporary

The Brat Next Door

Fantasy LitRPG

(Set in the same world as Guardians Of The Round Table Series)

Tales Of Inadon 1: The Disc (Co-written with Storm and Rhys Petersen) (short story in Game On! Anthology)

Post Apocalyptic Sci-Fi

Compulsive Directive

NONFICTION

A Year Of Weekly Writing Exercises (Creative Writing)

Cooking For Families With Allergies (Cooking) (Co-written with Storm Petersen)

Tell Me A Story, Grandma (Memoir)

For the most up to date details on available titles visit:

www.avrilsabine.com/books/bibliography

Demon Hunter Series

To learn more about the other books in this series visit:

www.avrilsabine.com/series/dh

BOOKS AVAILABLE IN THE DEMON HUNTER SERIES

Book 1: Blood Sacrifice

Book 2: Retribution

Book 3: Tainted

Book 4: Premonition

Book 5: Cursed

Book 6: Feud

Book 7: Extrication

Disclaimer

This is a work of fiction. Names, characters, businesses, places, events and incidents are either the products of the author's imagination or used in a fictitious manner. Any resemblance to actual persons, living or dead, or actual events is purely coincidental. The opinions expressed or beliefs held are those of the characters and should not be assumed to be the opinions or beliefs of the author.

www.ingramcontent.com/pod-product-compliance
Lightning Source LLC
Chambersburg PA
CBHW050757190726
48285CB00005B/1706